9 DOWN IS
DEAD

9 DOWN IS
DEAD

KENNETH L. TOPPELL

BROWN BOOKS
PUBLISHING GROUP

9 Down is Dead

Brown Books Publishing Group
Dallas, TX/New York, NY
www.BrownBooks.com
(972) 381-0009

A New Era in Publishing®

Publisher's Cataloging-In-Publication Data

Names: Toppell, K., author.
Title: 9 down is dead / Kenneth L. Toppell.
Other Titles: Nine down is dead
Description: Dallas, TX ; New York, NY : Brown Books Publishing
    Group, [2022]
Identifiers: ISBN 9781612545530 (paperback)
Subjects: LCSH: Chief executive officers--Fiction. | Serial
    murderers--Fiction. | Crossword puzzles--Fiction. |
    Inheritance and succession--Fiction. | Cousins--Fiction. |
    LCGFT: Detective and mystery fiction.
Classification: LCC PS3620.O587462 A19 2022 | DDC
    813/.6--dc23

ISBN 978-1-61254-553-0
LCCN 2021921918

Printed in the United States
10 9 8 7 6 5 4 3 2 1

For more information or to contact the author, please go to
www.KenToppellBooks.com.

For Michael, Josh, and Talia

They teach me how to be Papa
while we sip some wine
I kvell, as I watch them
Grown, loving, and fine

"*Do I rue a life wasted doing crosswords?*
Yes, but I do know the three-letter word for regret."
—ROBERT BREAULT

"*Baseball is a dull game only for those with dull minds.*"
—RED SMITH

"*Baseball is an eight-letter word.*"
—ME

PROLOGUE

B rad Groes had it all. OK, he was going bald, but except for that, he had everything. At least he did before he disappeared. He was twenty-nine years old and the CEO of a tech company he had founded, built, and then sold for over a billion dollars. He was a bachelor who didn't have to beg for companionship. But he took a few days off to be alone. He had a dilemma at work that needed sorting out. He told his office that he was taking a four-day weekend and would return the following Tuesday. Unfortunately, he didn't tell anyone where he was going. He could have gone anywhere from his Seattle home. Instead, he went somewhere. And that was the problem.

Groes had been making his own investment decisions since college, but he knew he couldn't keep it up. He and the company had too much cash now. He didn't have the time to study the market, and he knew he had a responsibility to his employees and his shareholders. That burden rested squarely on his shoulders. Even a rumor that he was interested in equities could affect the market. He needed a professional money manager, but he had no idea whom to trust. He handled the technology effortlessly. That was second nature to him. He was comfortable with technology. He wasn't comfortable with all that money.

That was how he found himself climbing the Pratt Lake Trail en route to the Granite Mountain Trail in the Mount

Baker-Snoqualmie National Forest. A mile or so further, he crossed an avalanche chute with a stream running through it, full blast with snowmelt. He continued up the rocky trail to the lookout sitting high above the rocks. The view was extraordinary. It was breathtakingly beautiful. He stood still, trying to take in everything before him.

He never took another step. The blow to his head was hard enough to generate an echo. He fell forward without uttering a word and disappeared into the canyon below.

CHAPTER
ONE

NOLAN HERBERT

I was in my office working on a crossword puzzle when the chairman of the board, Biltong J. Murworth, called an emergency meeting. No one had seen Brad Groes, the CEO, for two weeks. This wasn't typical of Groes, who was usually the first person in the office and the last one to leave. He hadn't even taken a vacation since he'd become CEO. Something was wrong. The board of directors was having a cow. If word got out, the stock price would tank. Thus, the crisis.

I didn't have many friends on the board. My support came from the outside directors, the members from other companies or public life. They brought expertise and prestige to the board and, therefore, the company. Rumor had it that my PhD stood for Phony Doctor, but, of course, that was just a rumor. I stayed in contact with this group, keeping them abreast of what they needed to know—and what I wanted them to know.

I'd also placed some phone calls to journalists, expressing doubt about the CEO's work. I happened to mention his absence during the conversations. These were informational calls only. Members of the Fourth Estate provide a valuable service. I was glad to lend a hand. Some people call this leaking; I call it public service.

I often made a point to take Murworth out to lunch. Not to curry favor, of course. No, I was simply getting to know the chairman better. The day of the board meeting, for example, was also a fine opportunity for me to have lunch with him. It was one of those little coincidences that seemed to mark my career.

"It's always good to spend some time with you, sir."

"Yes, I'm sure it is."

"Would you like a drink?" I asked.

"No, I have a great deal of work to do before the meeting this evening."

"Oh, of course. I thought you might want to relax a bit beforehand."

"Herbert, don't you have any work to do?" Murworth questioned me.

"Of course, I do. I was worried about you, that's all."

"Herbert, I've never actually seen you work. You do work here, don't you?"

"Sir? I don't know what you mean. I work here. I'm on the ninth floor," I said.

"So am I, yet I've never seen you there. Odd, isn't it?"

"Well, I do work here. I'm in the little office on the right at the end of the corridor." This wasn't going well.

"Herbert, that's the bathroom. Maybe we need to talk some more after the meeting." Biltong Murworth got up from the table. He walked to the door of the bistro and left, not looking back.

I remained seated while I wiped the sweat from my forehead and my heart rate returned to normal. I was not incompetent. No, not incompetent. I only appeared incapable of doing any original work. It was easier that way. I could work on a team, borrow, perhaps steal, from my colleagues, and smile all the while. I was good at it. That was how I had risen as far as I had. I was on the board, after all.

I was confident I had the support of the outside directors. They knew only what I told them about the company. The inside directors were more difficult. Some of them were aware of my work, though no one could remember my contributions. I'm the one who led the team to computerize Human Resources. Well, the guy from Cal Poly on the sixth floor did it, but I thanked him profusely, even though his name wasn't anywhere in our scope of work.

The big dogs were just itching for the chance to get rid of me. They were jealous of the publicity I got when I floated rumors about my successes at work or at play. I worked hard to keep my reputation afloat.

GDT was a technology company that dealt with agriculture. I was recruited because of my PhD. The lure for farmers was to keep their products contaminant free. That was my job. I was good at my job. There weren't any fuckups on my watch. That was the problem. It wasn't that I fixed the problems; I prevented them. Okay, I had others who did the leg work, but someone needed to be in charge, right? I decided that would be me.

If I could fuel enough doubt about Groes, I thought I could take him down. All those shares made my mouth water. They were voting shares. I still needed to be careful around those. If Groes wasn't found, I could add CEO to my PhD.

CHAPTER TWO

HENRY ATKINSON

I was reading about Moe Berg, possibly the most unusual baseball player of all time. Berg was surely a genius. He spoke seven languages, including Sanskrit, read ten newspapers a day, had degrees from Princeton and Columbia Law School, and studied philosophy at the Sorbonne. It was Moe Berg, once described as "Good field, no hit," who had his baseball card on display at the CIA and who was awarded the Medal of Freedom for his service as a spy during World War II.

This was what I loved to do. I was a retired attorney and a licensed private investigator. I had two passions in life—baseball and my wife Carolyn, a former journalist. I teased her that the ink still ran in her veins. She could smell a story.

I was deep into the book when I received a call from Stanford Wight, a friend from law school. There was the usual banter about each other's health, families, and activities before Wight got down to business.

"Henry, if I remember correctly, don't you know Randall Huntington?" he asked.

"Yeah. We're both on the Committee for the Environment of Northern New York. It's a small group, but we're very active."

"I thought I remembered that right. Listen, I need your help. You heard that Brad Groes disappeared, didn't you?"

"When a billionaire vanishes, it even makes the news in small towns, Stan," I said.

"I know, I didn't mean to insult you. But some notes of Brad's were found indicating that he had approached Huntington to manage his fund portfolio. Since Brad's disappearance, the stock price of GDT has fluctuated wildly, overall downward. The board wants to ask Huntington to be its new chairman, but nobody knows him personally."

"I assume then that you want me to speak to him. But first, what is GDT?"

"Sorry. That's Global Development Technologies. Brad was the founder and CEO," Stan told me.

"Why don't you promote from within, or someone known to the board?"

"The leading candidate to replace him so far is a guy named Nolan Herbert. Frankly, Henry, the board's counsel doesn't trust him. The executive committee won't confirm him except as the acting CEO until someone else is named. Jacoby, he's the lawyer, and I think that someone like Huntington has the clout and gravitas to get the company back on track. Do you know him well enough to approach him for us?"

"I do know him fairly well. But I'd rather have you make the offer. I'll get in touch with him and explain the situation. If he agrees to talk to you, I'll get you two together."

CHAPTER
THREE

NOLAN HERBERT

I sat in the front of the room. At least as close as I could. The seats nearest the very front were reserved for the executive committee. They were my major adversaries, my biggest problem. They had the real power, even more than Groes once he'd sold the company.

Chairman Murworth opened the meeting with a brief history of Groes's disappearance. A month passed since he had been seen. Then the chairman spoke about a mysterious leak to a reporter that Groes was missing. The market value of the corporation had taken a significant hit when that news reached the street, though the stock price had since stabilized. I kept my cool, but my heart was racing.

Apparently, only two people knew Groes's cell phone number. Neither that nor the landline was being answered. The board voted to have Groes's executive assistant go to Groes's home and report back to them. Balderdash. "Executive assistant"—a fancy name for secretary. Before the meeting adjourned, the chairman said that by the next board meeting he would also have a report on the person who had leaked the information about Groes's absence.

Amid the movement of chairs, subdued conversations, and momentary disorder of the end of a meeting,

I approached Murworth. "Sir, you did a masterful job, as always. How about a drink or some coffee?"

The chairman was an older man. This disruption of business as usual had taken a toll on him. He looked over at me with disdain but agreed to some coffee. He sat back down while I went to the two carafes that had been set up for the meeting. I poured two cups, one from each decanter, adding sweetener and cream from the ubiquitous little creamers found all over the building. I placed a cup in front of the old man and took one for myself.

As he began to drink, Murworth asked if his was decaf. "I can chair a meeting involving billions of dollars, but the doctors say I can't have caffeine. I've already outlived my cardiologist, but I don't want to push it."

"You're right, sir. Have mine. It's decaf." Before the chairman could object, I switched with him, knowing that the decaf had more than sweetener in it.

No one else was in the room. We sat quietly and drank our coffee. A few minutes passed before the elderly gentleman leaned forward. "I know it was you, Herbert. You leaked the story. Why?"

I looked thoughtful. I finished my coffee with a flourish. "Groes is not the only genius here. That's important to know. I'll take this place over and turn it around. Everyone will know that I rose to the occasion. Unfortunately, you won't. Rise to the occasion, that is. Or anything else."

The chairman of the board looked at me. Then he tried to get to his feet. He couldn't, and he became confused and angry. He muttered, "You goddamn son of a bitch." Then he fell back into the chair and died.

I yelled for help once or twice. No one was left on the "C" floor. I called 911 and walked to the elevator. Then I went to my office, which was not on the ninth floor like I had tried to convince the ornery old man. I worked on a crossword puzzle for a few moments. Later, I was back upstairs, where I was consumed with grief as the EMTs tried in vain to resuscitate the late chairman. *Grief* was Thirteen Down.

As the horde of officers, EMTs, and members of the ninth-floor ghouls and secretaries began to drift off, I took a walk along that corridor. I'd been there often. Soon, I wouldn't be a visitor.

CHAPTER FOUR

RANDALL HUNTINGTON

Morton Jacoby and Stanford Wight, Brad Groes' personal attorney, flew out to New York the day after Murworth's funeral. Henry Atkinson met them at JFK, and the three of them took a Priority One Jet charter to Ithaca. Henry drove the last eleven miles to Trumansburg where I was waiting in the den of Henry's house talking with Carolyn.

"Gentlemen, you have business to discuss which is way above our pay grade. We'll leave you to it. The coffee pot is on my desk. Carolyn has some sandwiches for you when you're ready," Henry said, pulling the sliding doors closed as they left the room.

He and Carolyn made themselves available for food and drink and, most importantly, directions to the bathroom. Inside the den, the three of us were trying to save a huge company and the jobs that went with it. Reputations were on the line, ours and everyone else who was connected to GDT. We worked, argued, deliberated, and reflected on the options and outcomes.

Morton Jacoby began by recounting the details of the board meeting that preceded their trip to give a picture of what I might face if I took the job.

"Within hours of Murworth's death, the board reconvened. The confirmation of Brad Groes's disappearance and the announcement of Biltong J. Murworth's death sent the share price of GDT into the toilet. The valuation of the company fell over 40 percent," Jacoby began.

"The board room was unnaturally quiet, despite perfect attendance, something no one could recall having happened before. The usual banter was missing. Murworth's death was sobering, but everyone knew that the future of the company was the real reason they were there.

"After vigorous debate and teleconferencing with the outside directors, Nolan Herbert, PhD, was named as acting CEO. Ralph Petersen, the chairman of the executive committee who became the acting chairman of the board, made the announcement to everyone assembled. The reaction was quick and loud. The anti-Herbert faction of the board began to walk out. I had to resort to using the gavel to get some form of order.

"I had to yell that, 'If you leave, ladies and gentlemen, remember that this meeting remains in session. New members can be added, and old ones may be asked to resign. Sit back down.' They were shocked into responding. Herbert and Petersen were confirmed, and the meeting adjourned without further ado," Morton Jacoby recalled.

Stanford Wight started the discussion by being blunt. "Mr. Huntington," he turned to address me, "GDT is in trouble. The board appointed an acting CEO, but Mort and I feel he will damage the brand. We believe the in-house board is behind us. Herbert has a hold on the outside directors, and that's depressing upper management. It's trickling down and affecting performance. He can't be allowed to have 'acting' removed from his title unless he is removed along with it."

I leaned forward on my elbows, staring in turn at Wight and Jacoby. "I understand the desire to be rid of Herbert, but I'm curious as to why he was appointed."

Jacoby spoke up. "The outside directors voted as a block. There was just enough support for him by other members that he was elected. We need you on the board. I can resign. Then, we can move to appoint you to fill my position. Herbert hates me. He may look at it as an opportunity to lessen whatever influence I have. Even an ignoramus like him will not be able to argue against your selection."

"Mr. Jacoby, don't hold back. Tell me how you truly feel," I said, smiling as I listened. I had retired as a director of The World Bank. I was accustomed to dealing with tyrants, dictators, and despots. Dealing with a directorate, not an individual, could pose a whole different set of problems.

After several hours, sandwiches, and beers, my curiosity was piqued. I was interested as long as I could meet with Wight and Jacoby behind the scenes. Wight explained that he was involved only as Brad Groes's attorney, but he would be available to serve as a sounding board. Jacoby explained that there were several members of the board that were trustworthy. They wanted to remove the acting CEO, but he had the outside board members eating from the palm of his hand. He needed only a few more votes to keep his job. If I became a board member, one of my tasks was to engineer Herbert's ouster.

When Carolyn came to get us for dinner, we were ready but surprised at how long we'd been there. She told us they'd taken our bags to bedrooms upstairs. Henry explained he'd made arrangements with the jet charter for an early morning flight to JFK where Wight and Jacoby would catch their flight to Seattle.

The next day, another flight took me to Albany, where my driver met me for the ride to my home in Saratoga Springs. I'd already decided to take the job. I felt that I owed it to Brad Groes, who had reached out to me to be the trustee of his estate. Given the circumstances, becoming a member of the board of directors would be the best way of doing just that. Jacoby seemed to be a bright guy, a good man to have as counsel. Herbert, on the other hand, looked to be something completely different.

CHAPTER
FIVE

NOLAN HERBERT

Three months later, the first regularly scheduled board meeting since Murworth's death was held. It was like all the others since I've been a member. It was dull except when I demanded that the "acting" be removed from my title. I received support once more from the outside directors, but nothing otherwise.

I preferred not to think of the "acting" title. I was thinking about weed, THC, Mary Jane. I had an opportunity to invest in marijuana in a big way. It would be a perfect merger partner for GDT, if the damn board removed the "acting" from my title. I wasn't above a little corporate horse trading. If all went as I planned, Brasoto would be a second-rate business when I was through. I must admit that I was unaware of the $63 billion merger with Geighter that would ultimately do away with the Brasoto name. Anyway, it didn't affect the production of Grounder, the world's top-selling herbicide. Details like that just got in my way.

Ganja seed, which was Grounder-resistant, could produce super crops. Of that, I was sure. I knew tests were being conducted, and the results would be presented soon. I'd make a killing. Unfortunately, the weeds being cultivated didn't contain tetrahydrocannabinol. These weeds were pests, garden, and farm nuisances. Weed containing THC was killed by Grounder. Sometimes I couldn't keep my weeds separate.

Several years previously, I'd bought into a small crop-dusting company. Over the next two years, I was able to buy the whole thing, including the planes. It was a legitimate business, albeit with a low profit margin. That was OK. I still made a good deal of money from my clients.

Occasionally, I substituted a little something of my own for the dusting. Then there would be a major die-off of the crop. I made personal visits to the unlucky farmers who had suffered so much. I was kindly and empathetic to their problems. I wanted to help them. Of course, I did. I offered them a simple deal. If they paid me a monthly fee, I'd be sure that their fields would not get poisoned. I'd protect them. Or they could sell their acreage to me.

Some of the farmers were angry; others were scared. When one of them threatened to call the police, I took note. I paid attention. I brought the poor man to my office to talk and have some coffee. Unfortunately, the apple farmer suffered a heart attack shortly after leaving the office. Monthly payments and sales picked up that very month, within weeks of the funeral.

The board meeting had the usual agenda—sales, progress in research protocols, employee turnover. That goddamn lawyer, Jacoby, asked me to leave so they could talk about the sexual harassment suit against me. This had been ongoing for several months, but tonight's discussion was brief. When I returned, the mood in the room was dark. The board had decided to separate itself from the suit. I would have to get myself a lawyer. GDT would settle the case on its own. Damn Jacoby. He was probably a Jew. He had a Jew name.

That bitch had sued me. That pissed me off. She was going to pay. She didn't know whom she was screwing. Had she just stayed the night, this would have all gone away. No, instead, she became Miss Goody Two Shoes. Well, she was going to learn, if I could just remember her name.

Before the meeting adjourned, Ralph Petersen, the chairman of the executive committee, announced the appointment of Randall Huntington as chairman of the board. Huntington's first action was to announce that human remains found in the Mount Baker-Snoqualmie National Forest had been identified as Brad Groes. I briefly sat up but slumped back in my chair. It wasn't anything I didn't know.

Next, Petersen announced an emergency earnings call for investors and financial analysts in the morning before the start of trading. He and Huntington knew they had to be proactive with the news of Brad Groes's death.

The exchanges called for a one-hour trading delay to assess the impact of the news. Despite Huntington's presence as chairman and the changes in the executive committee, the subsequent drop in the share price of GDT was dramatic. The market value of GDT was now less than 40 percent of its value before Groes disappeared.

CHAPTER
SIX

RANDALL HUNTINGTON

The share price of GDT stabilized after I gave several interviews to CNBC, *Bloomberg News*, and *The Wall Street Journal*. Ralph Petersen, the chairman of the executive committee, spoke to *The New York Times* and the *Financial Times*. Internally, the board was in continuous turmoil because of Herbert's behavior.

The executive committee of the board of directors ultimately held a closed-door meeting to discuss Herbert's continuing presence as the acting CEO—ostensibly to consider removing the "acting" title from Herbert's name. The meeting was really called because of speculation that he might be removed from the title instead. The market was reacting badly to rumors of such a move. The stability of the company was being questioned once again. After the collapse of the company share price when Brad Groes's death was confirmed, the board was taking this seriously. Any merger buzz had vanished. The talking heads on the street thought that a takeover was the only way the company would survive, but even the takeover bid price had been lowered dramatically.

As chairman of the board, I opened the discussion. "Nolan Herbert has proven, in the past two years, that he is incapable of running this company. Since I have been privileged to be your chairman, it has become evident to me that he is not fit for the position of CEO, or, in fact, any other position of responsibility.

"Nonetheless, I don't believe that we can summarily dismiss him. This company is a strong one, based on extraordinary technology. It has an exceptional workforce and strong leadership in all its divisions. However, it suffers from the belief that this is a one-idea company, and that idea was Brad's.

"Ladies and gentlemen, this isn't 'truck farming' we're talking about. We are more than that. GDT is not simply an example of applying technology to agriculture. We teach the farmer how to feed his crop. We assist him in restoring his soil. By educating him on the best time and place to plant, we increase his productivity. Then we provide storage and delivery for the fruits and vegetables.

"I believe that we must demonstrate the diversity in our product line. We must show off our people to reestablish our vigor.

"That doesn't mean we show off Herbert. We can't fire him right now, no matter how much he deserves it. Removing him at this time would invalidate all that we have to prove. I believe strongly that the company can run quite well without him, better in fact. But we must devote energies to fixing his mistakes and covering his misadventures. We must bide our time until letting him go confirms our value."

I sat down, opening the floor for comments. Arguments flew across the table. Nobody was in favor of keeping Herbert. The only disagreements were about when to let him go. Ultimately, my analysis was considered reasonable and won the day.

Members were assigned to oversee everything Nolan Herbert did henceforth. As it turned out, Herbert was rarely in the office. His job became mostly ceremonial. He was placed in charge of company picnics, holiday parties, and the quarterly dinner for the board of directors. He was encouraged to represent the company at international conferences, accompanied by members of the board who truly understood what the company did and kept Herbert out of trouble. Then he would spend a few weeks at his villa in the South of France. He believed strongly in fornication on vacation and practiced as often as possible. He was paid quite well for his vacation time, and he returned to Seattle with a good tan, relaxed, and ready to work, a frightening thought to members of the executive committee.

CHAPTER
SEVEN

Rachal Groes

I was in the conference room where I worked, across from an attorney named Stanford Wight. He had procured the room for this meeting from the executive assistant to the company's president when he mentioned that he was Brad Groes's lawyer.

I knew Groes dissapeared two years ago, as did most of the US and Canada. I also knew that I was somehow related to the missing billionaire, but I'd never met him. I didn't know anyone who claimed they had.

"Ms. Groes, thank you for taking the time to meet me. As I explained on the phone, I've been Brad's attorney for several years. When he disappeared—after the initial flurry of activity, searches, and publicity turned up nothing—I began to look for relatives. Brad had never mentioned any, except that his parents had died in a car accident. I used several sources to find that you and he were third cousins, once removed. That means he was the great-grandchild of your great-great-aunt or great-great-uncle. You share a set of great-great-grandparents with your third cousin, but do not have the same great-grandparents. I promise you that confused me as much as you are right now. I've got this set up in a genealogy chart for you to review." He handed me a chart from his briefcase.

"Thank you, Mr. Wight, but why is this necessary?"

"Because, my dear, you are his sole heir." He reached into the portfolio case once again and placed the death certificate before me. "Last week, a hiker in a national forest northwest of Seattle came across the remains of a body that DNA has identified as Brad Groes.

"He knew of your existence much as you did his. He also had no idea of how you were related, but his will leaves his estate to his 'nearest relative, Rachal.'" Wight then presented me with a copy of Brad Groes's will.

I couldn't say a thing. I looked at the death certificate, the ancestry chart, and the will. I shook my head in utter disbelief. There were no tears of personal loss. I didn't know the man. I had a lovely life working for a software development firm in Silicon Valley—a life that would be turned upside down. I had no idea how to be rich.

Wight got up to get me some water. I stared without focus at the bottle for what felt like an eternity. Slowly, I pushed errant strands of hair behind my ear and sat up.

I was in shock. Not the kind of shock that required intensive care, but the feeling of incredulity and emotional numbness that came from the news that I was now rich, richer than I could ever imagine. I sighed, stood, and walked to the windows which comprised one wall of the room. I looked out at a world I was afraid I would lose. Would I be able to go shopping by myself or go to lunch with friends? Would my wealth color all of my relationships from now on? I wrote software programs, for Chrissakes.

"Mr. Wight, I'm not a foolish woman. I'm not going to turn this money down. It's my inheritance, after all. I know it must be filed in court, but will it be open to the public? I'll become tabloid fodder, won't I? Paparazzi everywhere, not a moment for myself. Where can I go to hide?"

"Ms. Groes, yes, the will must be filed in court, but tabloids or any other news source will have to find it on their own. It's been over two years since Brad disappeared, and he's vanished from the news as well. The last will and testament will be filed in Skagit County, Washington, where the bones were located. Unless you plan on taking an active role in Brad's company, Global Development Technologies, you won't even be mentioned. The company has a new chairman of the board and an acting CEO. They're going to be the ones in the spotlight.

"As a matter of fact, Brad had originally reached out to Randall Huntington, a former director of the World Bank, to be his money manager. He's now the chairman and I feel certain that he would be quite discreet if you wanted him to handle that for you. The fact that you live in another state ought to work out for you as far as unwanted notoriety."

"Mr. Wight," I turned to face him as I leaned against the window. "Will you represent me as you did with Mr. Groes?"

"Of course. I would be honored."

"Thank you. My first request will be for you to ask Mr. Huntington to call me. I'd prefer if he calls himself, not through a secretary or assistant. That's one less person to know who I am. I will also need to learn how to access these funds. Now, if you would excuse me, I really must get back to work." I looked back outside for a moment, then turned and left the room.

I got to work every day at seven thirty. A group of early birds always joined me for breakfast. They were in their mid-twenties, recent graduates of West Coast tech incubators, like Stanford, UC Berkeley, and Cal Tech. I was considered a newbie to Silicon Valley, having gone to school on the East Coast.

I enjoyed my job. I enjoyed my colleagues. To some of them, I was something of a cipher, an unknown. Breakfasts could be raucous and rowdy. I was an enthusiastic participant. Once we got down to work, I could fix technical problems that were beyond the abilities of most of my colleagues. I would review their work and edit or correct it. I always refused credit. After work or on the weekends, I kept to myself. When I did go out, it was always in a crowd for birthdays, promotions, or engagements, things like that.

My female friends tried to fix me up to no avail. They teased me about which guy seemed to be smitten with me. I appreciated the compliments, but I kept my private life private. After a year or so, they seemed to accept me as something of a prodigy, eccentric and quirky as those folks often are. If I had someone in my life, no one at work was privy to that information.

I did indeed have a romantic interest, albeit unrequited. It was someone I met at school, Rensselaer Polytechnic Institute, outside Albany, New York. He'd become a criminal attorney in Seattle. I'd been a nerd at college, graduating in three years. He'd been a fraternity man, graduating in five years. I doubted that he even knew who I was, but hope springs eternal. Anyway, I hadn't met anyone interesting enough to attract me.

I went to Seattle to meet with Mr. Wight on a regular basis. He arranged for me to stay in a hotel near his office. Then I would meet with Randall Huntington.

This was how my new life began. I was terrified of the changes and the responsibilities that were required with wealth of this degree. There weren't any "How to Be Wealthy Beyond Comprehension" books. Over time, I became comfortable with this stealth life, but it was learning on the fly.

CHAPTER
EIGHT

NOLAN HERBERT

When I returned from an extended visit to my villa, I called Ralph Petersen, the chairman of the executive committee and the director of sales for the company. I thought we should have lunch together and get to know each other better. I could tell that Petersen wasn't thrilled by the idea but acquiesced if only to find out what was really on my mind. We agreed to meet at an expensive restaurant close to the waterfront. I was already seated when Petersen arrived.

"Good morning, Nolan. I see you've been very successful recently."

The waiter came by with the menus. Petersen sat and ordered iced tea, amused by my Vodka Manhattan. "Did you have a good time? I've never been to the South of France," Petersen said.

"It was terrific. You really must go."

The waiter returned with the iced tea and took our orders.

"Ralph, I've got some new ideas that I wanted to pass by you. I think we should get into the weed business."

"Well, Nolan, you realize that we work with both GMO and non-GMO farmers. They fight every day to keep weeds out. What they grow is their own business."

"Of course, of course. But I think we can change the business for everyone's benefit," I said.

"How do you mean?" Petersen was hesitant already.

"What if we could deliver weed by crop dusters?"

"Look, Nolan, buying seed is complex. For example, there are fifty to sixty varieties of corn or soybeans. Consider seed corn. The farmer must choose which variety based on how long it takes to mature. How tall does he want the stalk to be? Does he know what color the cob will be? What about disease susceptibility or root length? In what conditions will the seeds be planted? We haven't even considered herbicide resistance."

Even with a PhD, I was in over my head. Way over. All I wanted to do was make a killing. I wasn't even sure which one of us was confused. I still thought it was a great idea. Maybe later.

"There is one other matter. When am I going to be made the permanent CEO? I hate this 'acting' crap," I said.

"You must know that it's been on the agenda of every meeting. We're discussing that item again at our next executive committee meeting. The results will be announced at the board meeting."

"Shit, Ralph. That's not for another three months. We need to get a move on."

"Nolan, you need to get a grip. You're being paid handsomely. You have a terrific office. Unlimited vacation time. If you're feeling stressed, take some more time off. Try the north of France." With that, he took the check, got up, and left. I was pissed. I needed to unwind after Petersen walked out. I ordered a martini and put it on his tab.

CHAPTER
NINE

Rob Emanuel

I had a corner office on the eighth floor in my new firm, Bauer, Bartholomew, Birnbaum, and Braun, or BB and BB, as it was called by the employees, associates, and even partners with a drink in their hand. The view of Seattle was breathtaking. My office faced Mount Rainier. My professional life was going well.

On the wall in my personal office was a plaque with a letterhead I had made to let my clients, stalwarts in white-collar crime, know what I thought of their excuses— BPC and T: Balderdash, Poppycock, Claptrap, and Twaddle. My new partners didn't know.

I specialized in white-collar crime. In essence, my clients were sleazeballs, but they dressed nicely and paid well. Mort Jacoby practiced corporate law, as did the occupants of the other two corner offices, not close enough to me to catch anything.

My legal assistant and I were going over my schedule when Maryann Wilson, one of the senior partners, knocked on the door. She handled family and child welfare cases. Her office was one floor below mine. She didn't like her clients mingling with the eighth-floor gang, as she referred to us. I rose to greet her as she came in.

"Ms. Wilson, please have a seat. I'm honored that you came in to see me. What can I do for you? Can I get you something to drink?" I was still uncomfortable around the senior partners. I'd never been in a partnership before.

"First, call me Maryann. I'm Ms. Wilson in my office. And yes. I'd love a cup of coffee."

"Of course." I stepped over to the side table where I had a single-cup coffee maker. As I was fussing with the machine, she asked, "Do you always make your coffee?"

"Can't blame anyone else then, can I?" I laughed at myself and brought her cup to her on a tray with sweetener and cream.

"Thank you." She stirred in some cream and took a sip. "I don't want to take up too much of your time, but I have a question. I have a client who's getting the house in a nasty divorce. It's been going on for almost two years. She came in to see me a couple of days ago with a peculiar complaint. She is about to move back into the house and—"

"Excuse me. Did you say, 'move back in'?"

"Uh-huh. Each of them was demanding the house, and the judge said they both had to vacate until the divorce was finalized. He was afraid that there could be vandalizing if one party was in the house, but the other one was awarded it in the settlement. Very expensive home with property. Out on the other side of the Snoqualmie Pass, along I-90.

"Anyway, she showed me pictures of the house. There are huge bushes—huckleberry, we think—growing all over the grounds. I mean, these are much bigger than any huckleberry bushes I've ever seen. She's convinced the ex-husband did it," Maryann said.

"It's an odd story, that's for sure, but how can I help you?"

"Well, he, the former husband, swears he had nothing to do with it. For starters, he's been out of state, which we confirmed. I know he could have hired someone else to do this, but I'm not even sure what 'this' is. Is it illegal to plant on someone else's property? I'm not sure if there's a crime here."

I leaned back in my chair and shook my head. "If this is typical of the cases that you handle, I'm glad all I see is embezzlement and bank fraud. The only charge I can think of is trespassing. There wasn't any breaking and entering. Are there any fields nearby?"

"No."

"Well then, this wouldn't appear to be seed drift. The only problem is the nuisance value of cleaning these plants out. I suppose that would start the nastiness all over again," I said.

"These two hate each other now. I'm going to call the other counsel and see what we can work out. It's a very peculiar situation. Would you be willing to take this case? I'll handle the divorce but trespassing, seed drift, et cetera are not my area."

"If I think of anything, I'll let you know." I stood up, a little uncomfortable by the direction the conversation had taken.

She rose to leave. "Nice office."

After she left, I sat down. I started making notes on this odd divorce case. Then I read over what Mort Jacoby told me. I'd been invited to a meeting with him by Randall Huntington, which had aroused my interest. How would an ineffectual executive have enough sway to keep his job on a board? He didn't sound so bungling to me.

CHAPTER
TEN

NOLAN HERBERT

I was furious. I'd missed another executive committee meeting. They were ignoring me by scheduling their meetings in the morning. They knew I wouldn't attend morning meetings. The item to drop the "acting" from my title wasn't even on the agenda. I was beginning to think the title was meant to be permanent.

Ralph Petersen had recently stepped down as chairman of the executive committee. I went straight to Petersen's office to discuss the matter. I brought two coffees with me from my morning stop in the lobby coffee shop.

"Ralph, I know I don't have an appointment, but I want to talk with you. I need to get something off my chest."

"Nolan, please come in. Have a seat." Petersen rose to greet me, clearly surprised. I knew I was an unwanted visitor.

I began to sit but looked around first, trying to find a place to put the drinks. "Oh, I forgot. This one's for you. I hope you don't mind, I started to put sugar in, like I do to mine. There's not much." I offered the cup.

Petersen graciously accepted the drink, found a place on his desk for it, and sat down. "What can I do for you?"

"As you know, the executive committee didn't put my item on the agenda yesterday. Frankly, I'm pissed. What the fuck is going on?"

Petersen, an older man, was conservative in dress and manner. He paused before he spoke. "Nolan, you are aware, are you not, that I'm no longer the chairman of the executive committee? As the past chairman, I'm there as a courtesy only."

"Petersen, cut the shit. You've overseen the committee as long as I've been here. It was your idea to buy the company. You make that thing run."

"I'm going to retire next year. I'm on the committee only until they get a good candidate to run the sales department. Randall and I have discussed this, and we're in agreement." He took a sip of his coffee.

"Jesus Christ, I don't care about your retirement or the new candidates. I want the title fixed. I'm the CEO. Not the 'acting' anything." I slapped the desk, got out of my chair, and with a flourish, leaned over the desk and threw my coffee away. I was face-to-face with Petersen, inches away, violating the older man's space. "Fix it, dammit. Fix it." Spittle went flying. I left the office in a self-righteous swagger.

Petersen didn't move at first. Then he shook his head, took a sip from the coffee, and went back to work. He died soon after.

The death of Ralph Petersen at his desk shocked the entire company. He had been the longest-serving employee. He wasn't well known outside the company, but his loss was felt far beyond the executive suite.

I was beside myself with grief. I came in around ten as I always did, had some coffee, and did the crossword puzzle before going upstairs. I found police and EMTs milling around the executive offices. When I heard that Ralph had died, I was inconsolable. After the body was removed, I asked that everyone go back to work in Ralph's honor. Then I left to go to my other office. Ralph Petersen was no longer in my way.

Mourning was Twenty-four Across. The puzzle was filling up.

No one noticed my absence. No one in management even missed me. My absences were frequent, and I dearly welcomed them. The reaction of others simply didn't matter.

I was spending more and more time at my crop-dusting offices. I had a full-time crew of pilots dusting my properties, which were spread over hundreds of acres. The yield was huge and grew rapidly. Gangs of migrant laborers picked the fruit and then packed the harvest for distribution to the Northeast and Upper Midwest, especially Minneapolis-St. Paul, my old stomping grounds.

Ralph Petersen's death had gone as planned, giving me enough time to be out of the building by the time the old bastard was found. I needed that. Earlier that month the news broke that Randall Blake Huntington, the chairman of the board, had moved to Seattle. That was a downer. As soon as he'd arrived, he took a more direct hand in running the company. He was involved in everything. It assured me that I would continue to be the acting CEO.

I was unusually pleased with myself the next morning. Petersen's death had added to the glow of getting laid, which was usually short lived. This was different. The bimbo had given me a good idea. She was so stoned she forgot my name. That wasn't unusual and used to annoy me. This time she gave me an idea. Marijuana was a crop, just like wheat or soy. It needed to be harvested and then distributed to sellers. I'd never thought about the dynamics of cannabis farming. I could still sell to the Twin Cities area, which I believed was the hottest market for the crop in the United States.

I should stop trying to poison weeds and start to cultivate weed. Recreational pot was legal in Washington. Minnesota looked like it would be next to legalize it. I was so busy with GDT, I had forgotten—I had been buying enough land that I could plant a fortune in pot. It was good that my work with cannabis plants was going so well. And *weed* was Three Across.

CHAPTER
ELEVEN

RANDALL HUNTINGTON

I settled into my new office with ease. I loved old man Murworth, but I couldn't stand his office another day. I didn't need a fancy place. Just a new one. His office was a mausoleum. I gave an ultimatum: a new office, or I move out of the building. I had a long career in economics and banking, including that stint at the World Bank. I let management know that I could oversee the company from afar if I had to move out.

I had taken the role of chairman because Brad Groes had reached out to me before he died, but that was the extent of our relationship. My closest tie to the firm had been the former chairman, Biltong Murworth, an old friend who had passed away unexpectedly. Through Murworth, I had also been acquainted with Ralph Petersen. His death was a shock.

I called an early morning meeting of the senior staff. They arrived on time and apprehensive. This was their first meeting with the me since I moved to Seattle full-time. They knew quite a bit about me, but they didn't know me very well. They didn't know what to expect, but they soon found out. I could be genial, knowledgeable, and curious. I could be, but now I wasn't.

"Where is Herbert? Isn't he still the acting CEO?"

Everyone in the room shuffled their feet and wriggled in their seats, their eyes darting around anxiously.

"Did I ask a tough question? The CEO isn't here. I think that that's odd," I said.

"Randall, I'm Morton Jacoby. We've met before. I gave up my seat to get you onto the board. I was the corporate attorney at the time. As you're aware, Herbert is very odd. He never comes in before ten thirty. He claims it's 'Nolan Herbert Time,' the right time. In fact, when he does arrive, he does nothing all day anyway." Jacoby cleared his throat. "Except crossword puzzles."

There was absolute quiet.

"When Brad Groes disappeared, our stock price tanked," Jacoby continued. "We had to appoint someone quickly. The outside directors voted by phone and all of them endorsed Herbert. He's got a PhD, which stands for 'phony doctor' around here.

"Every time the board decides to get rid of him, something else happens. Bill Murworth died of a heart attack right after talking to Herbert. We kept Herbert on. Then Ralph Petersen, the former chairman of the executive committee, died after arguing with Herbert. Both times, the board refused to fire him or remove 'acting' from his title. He seems to have the outside board members wrapped up."

I was stunned. "This is absurd. Herbert is incompetent, and he's still the acting CEO. The chairman of the board drops dead after speaking with him. The chairman of the executive committee drops dead after arguing with him. I know that I once thought we couldn't fire him, but this is beyond acceptable. Am I the only one here who thinks this is strange?"

Nothing was said. The silence was overwhelming. I looked around the room. It was clear on their faces. A new chairman was in town.

"Morton, if you'll accept the job, you're the corporate attorney again, as of this moment. I want to speak with you after this meeting, on the q.t. If this company is to survive, we, the people in this room, must act. Morton, you are also the chairman of the executive committee until you select a new one from within. Now, the rest of you, go back to work. This meeting is over and confidential."

Jacoby was hesitant, but he stood up and said, "I have one condition. My friends call me Mort."

Three days later, I stood in front of Jacoby's home. I was with Stanford Wight, the new chairman of the executive committee. Gail Jacoby opened the door.

"Randall, Stan. How nice to see you. Please come in."

"Thank you," said Wight. "I believe Mort is expecting us."

"He's in the den. May I get you some coffee?"

"Thank you," I replied. "Mrs. Jacoby, I don't wish to be melodramatic, but this meeting never happened. Do you understand?"

"Absolutely. I'll be right in with the coffee." Gail led us to the den and left the room.

Jacoby rose to greet us. We got right down to business.

"Mort, we have a problem. First, why weren't you on the board or executive committee?"

"I wasn't invited back until the meeting three days ago. I resigned my seat to open it up when the board asked you to join. Herbert and his backers don't want me as the corporate counsel," Jacoby said.

"Well, Nolan Herbert is our problem. He contributes nothing. He's rarely there. I need to know how to get rid of him without damaging the company. I used to think we could manage him," I reflected. "I was wrong."

"Randall, you can get rid of Herbert. It'll have to be done carefully. He's a litigious son-of-a-bitch. I've seen the cases he's involved in. And you are aware of how much his departure might roil the market." Jacoby sat back, pensive, fingers steepled on his lips. His wife opened the door, brought in a tray of coffee, cups, saucers, a container of half-and-half, and a bowl of sweetener packets. She left without saying a word.

"Oh, for Chrissakes, once I had that exact thought. Not any longer. Now, I'm betting the market will be overjoyed if we get rid of him. But when he leaves, I want it to be ironclad," I said. Over the next three hours, ideas and coffee flowed freely. While I did not suffer fools gladly—or in any other way—my interest in saving the company was genuine. Jacoby and Wight felt empowered to speak candidly, and they did. It was an opportunity for Mort Jacoby to finally work with the board and not simply window dress. Stanford Wight was gushing with enthusiasm.

Over the next few weeks, I stepped up the meeting schedules for the administrative team. I met with Mort

Jacoby or Stanford Wight daily. The board meetings were moved to a monthly basis at noon. Morton Jacoby was officially added to the executive committee and the board. Nolan Herbert was invited only as a matter of protocol. I didn't care if he quit.

I had come around to the belief that the acting CEO should leave, one way or another. He was worse than a merely unfortunate choice for CEO. There was something malignant about him. Not for a nanosecond did I believe that Herbert was the blundering doofus that he portrayed himself to be. People died around him. He kept to a schedule, even if it was on Nolan Herbert Time. This wasn't a silly comedian. Herbert was an evil clown, goddammit.

I had my secretary pull Herbert's personnel file. Might as well start at the beginning. It should have been done long ago. She was tasked with checking all the work and educational history they had on Herbert in human resources. In the meantime, I wanted Herbert kept on a tight leash. Someone Jacoby or Wight selected had to accompany the acting CEO at all times; better yet, I wanted a private investigator.

The next time I broached the idea of looking into the wretched CEO, Jacoby spoke with me after the meeting. He let it be known that his law partner, Rob Emanuel, had his investigator looking into everything about Nolan Herbert.

"Is he any good, this investigator?"

"I don't know him, but he works for Rob personally. I'm comfortable with that," Jacoby said.

I thought it over for a moment. "Good." Then I went back to my office.

CHAPTER
TWELVE

RACHAL GROES

Randall Huntington kept working as my money manager. He made a point of keeping to our schedule, meeting with me every three months. I'd become seriously wealthy over the years; he'd committed to keeping it that way. I always met with him in Seattle. He was now well known as the chairman of the board at GDT. He was a familiar customer to the maître d' at many of the finest restaurants in town. After a meeting in his private office, he would accompany me to dinner. I'd leave the following day.

My life and career had blossomed since my inheritance. I was relaxed, more confident at work. I still lived in a modest cottage in Palo Alto, but I think I dressed a little better, and I began to wear some jewelry. My private life remained private. There was always a whisper that I was a lesbian, but no one had seen me out with anyone of either sex. My co-workers accepted me as unconventional.

One weekend, when I was in Seattle for my regular meeting with Randall, he called me at my hotel.

"Rachal, how are you?"

"I'm fine, Randall. How are you? You've never called me here. Is everything alright?"

"I'm a bit tired, I have to admit. I have your report prepared, but I've been in meetings almost continuously since yesterday morning. We've had some problems at GDT that have required my full attention."

"Do you need to cancel our meeting?"

"I'm afraid I'll have to, but I still want to have dinner with you. I think you should know what's going on here. As a matter of fact, it's important that you do," Randall said.

"All right. I'll see you at the rooftop dinner club at the hotel. Our usual table."

I sensed his relief. I was the major shareholder in GDT. I needed to be kept in the loop even though I was beneath the radar. Ralph Petersen's death was another blow to the company's stability. He decided to ask Mort Jacoby to join us. Mort had been named the corporate counsel. It was time I met him.

I dressed conservatively. Not prudish, not really "modest," but simply and with style. In the two years that I had been working with Randall Huntington, I had not heard him sound like this. Nor had dinner been anything but pleasant conversation and anecdotes from Huntington's past.

When I arrived, I was seated and a glass of pinot grigio was brought to the table. The chairman introduced me to the corporate attorney, Mort Jacoby. Both men already had drinks.

"Rachal, I know this is a departure from our usual routine, but I think that you should know of some developments at GDT. Mort, this young lady is our largest stockholder, Rachal Groes."

I smiled and nodded to the surprised lawyer. He finished his drink and signaled for another.

"Groes, as in Brad Groes?"

"I was his closest relative."

"I'm so sorry. Did you two know each other?" Jacoby asked.

"No. His attorney, Stanford Wight, tracked me down when the remains were identified."

"I know Wight. Good man. He's now the chairman of our executive committee." Jacoby had reclaimed his equanimity.

"The reason I wanted you to meet Mort has to do with your voting power." Huntington was bringing the conversation back where he wanted it. "We have a big problem, Rachal. There have been three deaths that deeply affected the board and the company's future.

"Brad's death was the first. Then came the former chairman of the board, Biltong Murworth, and recently, Ralph Petersen, the most senior member of the board. These have occurred over almost two-and-a-half years. As a matter of fact, that's why I was brought in, after meeting Mort and Stanford.

"The board appointed a man named Nolan Herbert as the acting CEO after Brad disappeared. The man is inept. In fact, we keep him away from anything important. Now he's demanding to have 'acting' removed from his title. He wants to have a larger role in the activities of the company," Randall said.

As Randall was speaking, Mort noticed that the selfsame Herbert was sitting alongside the windows and got my attention. Nolan was sitting across from a woman, looking down her blouse. Classic. Mount Rainier and the young lady both had prodigious projections. Nolan was ignoring Rainier's. The woman was ignoring him.

"He has the outside directors eating out of his hand. If any one of the inside directors is absent from a board meeting, he could literally have the votes to take over. GDT cannot countenance that. Only your voting power can change the dynamics. I know that you've wanted to be as anonymous as possible, but we need your help," Randall said.

Jacoby nodded in the direction of Herbert. Both gentlemen looked at me, waiting for my answer.

It had been close to three years that Randall and I were working together. He had navigated my path to affluence in secrecy. Only three men knew who I was or anything about me. All three were intimately involved with GDT. I looked over to the table where Nolan Herbert was ogling his dinner partner's chest. Good Lord.

It was time for me to put my big girl pants on.

"Gentlemen, shall we eat?" I smiled, and a waiter was at my side.

CHAPTER THIRTEEN

STANFORD WIGHT

Henry Atkinson was writing a book. Not a legal opinion, but a book. *The Seattle Pilots: One Year in the Mist*. Not many people know about the Pilots, that, of course, being one of their problems. They were a dreadful Major League Baseball team for one year. I don't mean they were bad one year. They were a team for one year. Literally, one year. They didn't improve, and they left town. Turnout had been terrible, which might have been a blessing, as they finished last in their division, though other teams had worse attendance. But they went bankrupt that misbegotten year. Then, they were sold and moved to Milwaukee six days before the first pitch was thrown the following season, with barely enough time to change "Seattle" to "Milwaukee" on their uniforms. Henry felt compelled to tell their story.

As a baseball aficionado, he knew the saga well. It was odd, quirky, and strange. He'd read everything he could about the team and the maneuvering to save it. It was time to get a personal feel for baseball in Seattle before Microsoft, Starbucks, and Amazon were there. Two minutes into a prepared presentation to his wife, Carolyn, she interrupted to suggest they go to Seattle. He kissed her and went to make reservations while she started to pack.

That's who they were. Henry's life as a patent attorney was a distant memory. His head was in the clouds. His mind was always on baseball, especially from the past. He was known by his classmates as a klutz in a china shop. Yet he had attracted Carolyn, a beautiful woman with a retro flair. She was stylish and slender, a word not used anymore. Pre-Henry, she had been a journalist and then a personal assistant to the publisher.

Sometimes, she had to repair Henry's tracks. Like when he woke me because he had forgotten the time difference. Then he called to apologize because he had forgotten the time difference. Carolyn called later in the day. Her apology stuck. Henry and I remained friends, though it seemed that I did like Carolyn more.

I made plans for us to get together and recommended where she should stay. I told Carolyn she could even bring Henry.

It was after seven. I was still in my office. Thinking about that episode with Henry took my mind off what I was reading. I sipped a whiskey while I read the Skagit County coroner's report on the bones identified as the late Brad Groes. I read the report slowly, as I had the first fifty or so times over the last three years. The coroner had called in a forensic anthropologist who had, in essence, written the report.

The skull had been smashed posteriorly and with an upward projection. This couldn't have occurred in a fall. There weren't any bone breaks noted on the forearms or hands, as in defensive mode, just random breaks reflecting a helter-skelter fall of an already dead body.

The conclusion was that this was murder. So far, I'd been able to keep the death considered an accident. If Rachal Groes's involvement with GDT became public, I wasn't sure if I could keep the lid on.

It shouldn't make any difference, but it would wake up the doubters and conspiracy theorists. The stock would tank again. I knew that was true. But who killed Brad Groes?

I poured myself another snifter and reached for the phone.

"Mort, it's Stan Wight. We need to talk."

I explained the circumstances of Brad Groes's death and my role in keeping it under wraps. I had promised Rachal Groes to try to keep her out of the public eye, but if she assumed a larger role at GDT, that would be impossible. The resulting publicity would likely make uncovering Brad's killer even more difficult.

Maybe Henry's visit could be beneficial. If the stories I'd heard were true, the klutz in the china shop had turned into a very effective investigator.

CHAPTER
FOURTEEN

Rob Emanuel

Maryann Wilson was waiting when I returned to the office. I was surprised to find her there. Except for a meeting of the partners, I hadn't seen her recently.

"To what do I owe this nice surprise?" I walked around my desk to my coffee machine. "Care to join me?"

"No, but thank you. Do you remember when I spoke to you about that divorce settlement where the house was awarded to the wife, but someone was growing these huge huckleberry bushes on her property?"

"Sure. You were going to speak to the other lawyer about the husband possibly being at fault," I said.

"Exactly. Well, the ex-husband had gone nowhere near the place, and while those plants were removed, there are even more there now. The last time these seed packets were dropped was the day before yesterday. The ex-husband happened to be there at the time. His ex-wife had asked him over, and the judge approved the visit since the divorce was final. Doreen was convinced someone was trying to drive her crazy.

"While he was there, a low-flying plane passed overhead and then came back around. They both saw things falling out of the plane into the yard. He got pictures of the markings on the plane. Then she picked up some of the items that had landed on her property," she said.

I was fascinated by the story. Now they had a case. This was trespassing at the minimum, in the first degree, along with inference of intent to commit a crime.

"Do you have the photos and whatever was being dropped?"

"Right here." She opened her purse and took out two photos. Then she handed me a sealed plastic bag, with what looked like seeds inside. "To this attorney's eyes, they look like seedpods. Unfortunately, I have no idea."

"Let me see them. I think we should get them to Washington State University. The markings on the plane should get us identification. I'll get on that immediately. Let your client know she has another mouth to feed. And I'm looking forward to making someone else pay."

She left the samples and the photos with me. I sent a request to the federal aircraft registry with the data from Maryann's photographs. Then I sent an inquiry to WSU on how to handle the samples. The story I'd just heard sounded more sinister than simple error or even mischief. It sounded like intent, but why? I was feeling good about the hunt.

CHAPTER
FIFTEEN

NOLAN HERBERT

Jack Dalton was right to be worried. He had seen those people taking pictures of the plane as he made his second pass over that damn house. The woman in the yard was even picking something up off the ground. He knew I wanted to own those last two properties. Dalton was only following orders: get that land. Well, at least the flyover of the other house went well. Two goddamn houses and it was his luck that somebody took his picture. Shit. He even told me how worried he was that I would be in today.

Dalton continued to have bad luck. I was there and wanted to review the flights. "Mr. Dalton. You're first today. How'd everything go?"

"Not bad, sir. The weather was good. Most of the deliveries were spot-on. The crop seems to be progressing well. The older deliveries should be ready for picking very soon."

"Not bad doesn't mean that everything went well, does it, Mr. Dalton? What went wrong?" I asked.

"Well, sir, on one of the two properties you want, there was a small problem."

"A small problem isn't bad. Of course, I'll be the judge of that, won't I, Mr. Dalton? What happened?"

"As I came back over to drop the excess cargo, a couple ran out of the house, and the guy took pictures of the plane. The woman was picking up samples as I left," Dalton said.

"I see. Mr. Dalton, why don't you stay after the meeting for some coffee. We can talk?"

Dalton simply nodded.

The rest of the meeting went well. The fields that I'd bought were coming along fine. Most of them had pot ready to be picked. Shipments to the Upper Midwest would begin within the week.

After the other pilots left, Dalton stood, waiting for me. I was making notes and calculating my initial shipments. When I finished, I motioned for Dalton to follow me.

We went back into the small room that I used for my private office. I took out some sweetener and put it into the cup for Dalton, nothing in my own cup. I made the coffee in one of those single-cup machines that are all the vogue. I carefully gave Dalton the one with sugar.

"Mr. Dalton, how long have you worked here?"

"A little over a year."

"Did you like working here?"

"Yes, is—Mr. Herbert, you said 'did' I like working here? Did you just fire me? I'm sorry about today. It won't happen again."

"Mr. Dalton, I'm sure it won't. Why don't you finish your coffee and relax a bit? Then take your plane back to Bellingham. I'll call ahead to make sure you have a ride home."

"Thanks, Boss. I was worried at first. I didn't want to disappoint you."

"Dalton, you have nothing to worry about." He took his coffee to-go.

That evening a plane crashed into Bellingham Bay. Witnesses were quoted as saying the pilot appeared to be trying to land.

The morning paper led with the story. A small plane had gone down in Bellingham Bay during an approach to the airport. The pilot's body was in the plane when it was brought to shore. The Federal Aviation Administration and the National Transportation Safety Board were handling the investigation, according to the Whatcom County Sheriff.

I was having my morning coffee in our building's Starbucks. I was reading the paper, about to start the crossword puzzle. I chuckled that *scone* was Seven Down. It had to be a subliminal suggestion when my phone buzzed.

"Herbert." I loved answering the phone that way.

"Nolan Herbert?"

"Yes. Who's calling?"

"Sir, this is Officer Bradshaw, Whatcom County Sheriff's Office. Do you own a small plane, a Beechcraft Bonanza?"

"I think our company does. Is something wrong?"

"A Bonanza registered to you was pulled out of Bellingham Bay late last night. The pilot Jack Dalton was found dead in the aircraft," Bradshaw said.

"That's terrible. Jack was a good man. He'd been with us for years." I wadded up the wax paper and missed the trash can again. "Shit. Sorry, that really is bad news. Can the plane be salvaged?"

"That's not my call, sir. You should check with the FAA on that. I'm trying to get in touch with Mr. Dalton's family for notification. Do you have that information?"

"Well, not with me, but my HR department will get in touch. Thanks again."

"The autopsy will be later today, Mr. Herbert. Will your aviation department need the results?" Bradshaw asked.

"Oh, of course. Thanks again, Detective." All I had were crop dusters. I didn't need any aviation department.

"It's Officer Bradshaw, sir, of the Whatcom County Sheriff's Office. Have a nice day."

We both hung up.

I was pleased with myself and decided I'd earned that extra scone. I knew I was called "phony doctor" at work, but I was for real. My PhD in biological sciences was from Minnesota State University in Mankato. I had a great time there. It was just three guys working together. I felt awful that the others didn't get their degree. They left school so suddenly. I still have the pictures of the two of them canoodling behind the watch tower.

My specialty, although I kept it under wraps, was environmental toxicology. I knew a great deal about toxins. Now, with what I'd learned about cannabis, I felt terrific. I knew how to remove roadblocks. Yes, I did.

I finished the crossword puzzle before I got to the office. *Bastard* was Twenty-two Across.

CHAPTER
SIXTEEN

Rob Emanuel

Spencer Granady was my investigator. He was an eccentric private cop who wore a fedora while working, if you can believe it. It was as if he wanted to be Sterling Hayden or Robert Mitchum, tough guys from the forties and fifties. Unfortunately, he was built like Dustin Hoffman. I thought it was a gag the first time we met. The fact was that most people he investigated had never heard of either of those old-time movie private investigators, but the peculiar detective proved to be effective, and he stayed in the background when necessary.

Several days previously, I'd gotten a call from my contact at the FAA. The plane I had asked about was identified as the one that had gone down in Bellingham Bay recently—the same day it was seen dropping invasive seed packets in the yard of Maryann Wilson's client.

My secretary got the Whatcom County Sheriff's Office on the phone. They wouldn't release the name of the pilot, as the family hadn't yet been notified, but she was able to get the name of the plane's owner. That was enough. There was something about this strange case that intrigued me. I might've had to devote more time to it, but I wanted to see it through.

I called Spencer to sic him onto Nolan Herbert. I could now relate Maryanne Wilson's case to the CEO of one of the largest corporations in the Pacific Northwest. This didn't make any sense to me. Was it coincidence that the plane in the bay was owned by Nolan Herbert? Christ. I don't believe events like these are random accidents. Spencer was going to help me prove it.

Then I called Mort Jacoby, my senior partner, but more importantly, the corporate counsel at GDT. I needed to let Mort know that the CEO of GDT was currently the subject of an investigation into a pilot's death. That inquiry was going to be done by my investigator.

It was almost seven o'clock. I was due at the selfsame Mort Jacoby's house in eight minutes. Whoops. Sometimes you've just got to hustle.

After I pulled up and surrendered my car to a valet (God, I hope he has a driver's license), I followed a well-dressed young woman to the house.

"Hi, I'm Rob Emanuel. I see that I'm not the last person to arrive." I held the door for her.

"Thank you. I hate being the last to walk in. I'm Rachal Groes."

Before I could respond, Mort Jacoby welcomed us. Rachal went on in and said hello to Randall Huntington as Mort pulled me aside.

"Rob, do you know who that was? That's Rachal Groes."

"I thought that's what she said." I looked at her speaking to the other guests. "She looks like a regular person, Mort. Attractive, poised, and very pretty."

"She's also very smart. Must run in the DNA. Anyway, what'd you need to talk to me about?"

"Can we talk in your den?" I asked.

"Of course. but aren't you're being somewhat melodramatic?" He pointed out the den and went to get me a glass of wine.

He found me looking at the book titles on his shelves.

"Mort, you read mysteries? This is a nice collection."

"Yeah, they're my guilty pleasure. I have my law books everywhere at the office. I don't like bringing that stuff home," Mort said.

"Maybe you can use those skills now. This is why I didn't want to speak in public. Maryann Wilson asked for my opinion about a case she was handling. Someone was dropping seeds around the house of one of her divorce clients. Literally buzzing the house and surrounding property while laying down seed packets. The last time it was done, the ex-husband took some photos of the plane. I checked with a buddy at the FAA, and the plane is owned by Nolan Herbert, the acting CEO of GDT."

My convivial host turned grim. He finished his Scotch in one swallow.

"Later that same day, that plane crashed into Bellingham Bay. The pilot was dead. I'm not sure if he died in the crash. The sheriff hadn't notified the family yet, so it's just a feeling."

"Are you implying that Herbert had something to do with the pilot's death?" Mort said.

"Don't jump to that conclusion. I'm not. He could have had a heart attack or thrown a blood clot. I'm just saying that I got the impression that he may have died while flying. Maybe that's why the crash occurred. I thought you ought to know about the Herbert connection."

Mort was refilling his glass from the decanter on the corner of his desk. "Rob, I want you to sit next to Randall Huntington. He's our chairman. Let him know what you've told me."

Seated across from me was the delightful creature who walked into the house with me, Rachal Groes. She was dressed in the ubiquitous little black dress and wore a chunky turquoise necklace. Except for small diamond studs in her ears, she wore no other jewelry. I noticed she didn't have a ring.

CHAPTER
SEVENTEEN

HENRY ATKINSON

I made plane reservations, first class from JFK to Sea-Tac. Thousands of points were required, but Carolyn and I had been collecting them for years. We hadn't ever flown in front of that damn curtain. Thanks to this mileage, we were going to see how the other half flew. Well, how another twelve to sixteen people flew. Carolyn found us a hotel downtown, and we added a rental car.

The drive into Seattle was interesting. We passed Boeing on the left and saw Mount Rainier on the right. Downtown Seattle was big but easy to cross as we found our lodgings without difficulty. After checking in, we went looking for Sicks' Stadium, or what was left of it.

The stadium had been the home of the little-lamented Pilots. It had also been the site of Seattle's minor league team, as well as the Negro Baseball League team, and was supposed to be torn down for a freeway extension. Only seating seventeen thousand fans, it had no running water after the seventh inning, forcing the players to shower at home or at the visiting team's hotel. Many observers thought that putting a team in a stadium named Sick was a foreboding sign. It's now the site of a large hardware store.

We took pictures of the store inside and out. The only known Pilot memorabilia was available in a showcase at the site of the old pitcher's mound inside the store. After talking with store employees, none of whom were old enough to remember the Pilots, we went back to the hotel.

It was eight o'clock before we felt like having dinner, given the time change from New York. We went down to the dining room in the hotel where we ordered, had a drink, and saw Stan Wight. He and his wife were sitting by themselves, nursing coffees. He'd checked with the hotel to see when our reservations were. Stan saw us first and stood to get our attention. I was glad to see an old friend but afraid that he'd remember my early morning gaffe.

I'd never been back to a law school reunion, so my reputation had grown in absentia, especially my role as an investigator. According to the alumni legend, I'd been shot and had been a shooter, run off with a beautiful woman, and partnered with a hitman. As it's said, "When the legend becomes fact, print the legend." What was legend and what was fact with me? I left that for someone else to decide.

We hadn't seen each other since I introduced him to Randall Huntington. He smiled and stood as he saw us approach the table. He introduced us to his wife, and, over the next few hours, dinner, and two bottles of wine, the four of us discussed the murder of Brad Groes. Groes's attorney described the findings of the forensic pathologist and explained why he'd kept the likelihood of murder from the press.

I couldn't get over how little was known about Groes's death. He'd disappeared about five years ago. He was only twenty-nine years old at the time of his death and worth over a billion dollars. I was surprised that there had been so little learned in that time despite the victim's prominence.

"You're right. No one knows anything. Part of that has to do with where he was killed, and part to do with the blackout I kept on publicity. He was my client. His company has been in jeopardy, along with every employee and investor," Wight said. "Henry, the police couldn't turn up a damn thing. Rachal Groes is Brad's only known heir, and with Randall increasing her role in the company, I'm afraid the hunt for Brad's killer will get lost in the shuffle.

"It's long past time to find out who killed Brad. I hope you can do it."

I called for the waiter and asked for another bottle of the wine Stan had ordered. Without my cousin Shelley, I was more likely to whine than know a decent bottle of wine on my own. He always knew what to order and where to eat. He and his wife, Marian, ran a coffeeshop and bookstore back in New Hampshire. He was also a retired hitman with very tough standards. He only cleaned out the riffraff.

"Stan, I appreciate your proposal. I do. But Carolyn and I are on a working holiday. We've never been here before; we're tourists. And we came to research a book I'm writing about the old Seattle Pilots."

"That's perfect, Henry. Tell anyone who asks that's what you're here to do. It keeps you unnoticed," Stan said.

"Does Randall know that you want to hire us?" Carolyn was hooked. She could smell the story. "Would Henry and I be working for you or the corporation? That'll make a big difference in our access to the board members. Who'll know about us?"

"As of right now, you'll both be working for me. You met Morton Jacoby when we were at your place interviewing Randall. Randall has appointed me to the board and brought Mort Jacoby back as corporate counsel. Mort and I have worked on many cases over the years."

Carolyn had been making occasional notes. "We need to meet with Randall and Mort. They'll be the ones to give us the access we'll need. But it's up to you, Stan, to let them know why we're here."

I hadn't said anything. "Carolyn, Stan. I don't want to do this. I'm a baseball fan. I love baseball stories and the way baseball and history interact. That's why we came here. That's what I want to do. Tell a story about a woebegone team at the height of the Vietnam War and the growing resistance movement. Baseball and history. I'm sorry." I stood up and waited for Carolyn to follow. No one else said anything.

CHAPTER
EIGHTEEN

ROB EMANUEL

I enjoyed the meal at Mort's home. I had a chance to speak with Randall Huntington. More than that, I was able to spend some time with Rachal Groes. She'd been talking to the chairman when Mort introduced me to the other guests.

The fact that my specialty was white-collar crime led to stale jokes and mild discomfort, but dinner began soon enough, and people dispersed to their seats. I was seated next to Randall Huntington and across from Rachal Groes.

I wanted to learn everything I could about Nolan Herbert. The smell coming from the "phony doctor" was rancid. I made my living defending people accused of crimes. Unfortunately, most were bad guys, sometimes very bad guys. They deserved representation, however, and I was good at it, even when I had to hold my nose when doing so. The chance to help the innocent escape unwarranted charges was why I accepted the shady, the disreputable, and the guilty as clients as well.

Everything I knew about Herbert was corrupt, crooked, and cruel, but I couldn't go to the US attorney's office yet. My career was based on beating them in court. Before I could take this case to Earl Sedlik's office, I needed more substantial evidence than the fact that three men had fatal heart attacks after meeting with Herbert. That's why I had called my investigator.

The conversation flowed as easily as if we were old friends. When I mentioned that I had graduated from Rensselaer Polytechnic Institute, she wasn't surprised. It was her alma mater as well, and it was hard-core math and science. I asked when she was there, but she smiled and reminded me that a gentleman didn't try to guess a lady's age. I grinned and agreed but still ventured the opinion that I must have gone there several years before she was a student. I never recognized her from school.

That alone explains why it took me so long to graduate. I was out to lunch. That I missed this girl speaks volumes to my collegiate condition. She was not quite five foot four, so she always wore heels, she said. She had dark hair, more auburn than black, with glittering black eyes. She radiated a restrained glamor.

"I was more of a nerd than the average student," she explained. "I honestly thought that one day someone would find out I didn't belong. So I hit the books and hid out the entire three years I was there."

"You graduated in three years? From RPI? Seriously? I was so scared there, I switched from games and simulation arts and sciences to philosophy. I thought it was, well, games. I ended up there for five years simply catching up. Getting into law school was a bitch—excuse the expression, because they all wanted to know why it took me so long to get out of college." Even Randall Huntington was tickled by that.

By the end of the evening, I was besotted.

I stood by my office window. I was facing Mount Rainier, but I didn't see a thing. My busy law practice had become overwhelming since I'd moved and joined the firm. It seemed like every sleazy white-collar slime ball on the West Coast had my number in their contacts list. That was redundant, but how else can you describe slime balls? They're sleazy.

It wasn't my work. I knew what I could and would do with my cases. I was stressed. I hadn't been stressed since I was in college. My reputation and income had grown substantially. I had a staff of four at the firm's office, as well as an independent investigator whose agency was off the premises, to keep our association out of sight. As I thought about the strange case of the plane that was dropping seeds on private property, I knew I needed to call Spencer Granady again.

Granady wasn't very big and never inspired fear, but the peculiar detective proved to be effective and stayed in the background when necessary. To me, Granady was more like a polecat, solitary and always busy burrowing for facts.

I was a defense attorney. This case was bizarre and needed looking into. I didn't have a dog in the fight at GDT, but Herbert was enmeshed in it. Anything that Spencer and I found would be turned over to my partner Mort Jacoby.

I called Spencer and set him onto Herbert. Then I called Rachal Groes. I'd been thinking about her for weeks. I wanted to talk to her. I hoped to see her.

Feeling only slightly better after my call to Spencer, I made myself some coffee. I had some time before my first appointment of the day. There was enough time to work out how to call a billionaire. One doesn't just call someone like that. Although they more than likely could answer the phone like other people, the caller should have something to say. I thought maybe I should make notes first.

No, she'd know I was reading or had memorized a speech, which was not a good idea. I recalled my first date, when I memorized what I needed to say. I called, and I thought she answered the phone. I remembered everything I had memorized that day. "Hi how are you do you want to go to the prom?" The girl answered, "Rob, wait a minute. Judy's upstairs. I'll get her." I had asked my intended date's sister to the prom.

I knew I was better than that now. I decided to wing it. I picked up the paper I had written her number on and dialed.

"Groes."

"Rachal, hi. This is Rob Emanuel."

There was a pause, then, "It's been a while. How are you?"

"It's been too long. I'm stressed out in general and terrified right now." I was glad she couldn't see me.

"What's wrong? Can I help?" she asked.

"Yes. Can I come down and see you this weekend? I'll understand if you say no. There's no excuse for my not calling sooner. I'm sorry if I bothered you. Maybe I'll see you when you're in Seattle and visiting Gail and Morton. You take care, bye."

"Don't hang up." Probably the quickest response she'd ever made. "Are you still there? Rob, hello?"

"Yes, I'm still here."

"Good. You know you sounded like a teenager asking for a date when he finally had a driver's license." She gave a little laugh.

"Well, it so happens that I would love to see you again. Let me know where and when, and I could meet you there," I said.

I finally took a breath. "You know that teenage kid who just got his license? Well, he's started breathing again, and he would love to pick you up. Whoops, I gave away his identity, didn't I? Rats. Well, I'll be there at six on Friday evening if that's good with you."

"It's fine. Do you have my address?"

"Got it from Morton. See you then." I felt better than I had in months.

CHAPTER
NINETEEN

Rachal Groes

At six o'clock Friday evening, Rob got out of a rental car holding flowers and a small, square package. As he approached the door, he carefully tucked the flowers under his arm so that he could ring the bell. I'd been watching from the sidelights. I opened the door before the sound of the chimes stopped. We looked at each other without saying a thing for a moment.

I felt myself blushing as I finally invited him in. "Are those for me?" I asked when he stepped into the room and remained speechless, as if he wanted me to hold the flowers for a neighbor.

It was his turn to blush and stammer as he handed his offerings to me. "The package is candy. I hope you like chocolates."

He looked just like I remembered from college. Tall, lanky, completely unaware of the effect he had on women. He had a slightly lopsided smile which made his eyes crinkle just so. He still had a full head of hair which was always in need of cutting.

I took the flowers to the kitchen and cut the tips off the stems. I put water in a vase with the flowers. I wanted to hug Rob Emanuel. I wanted him to put his arms around me and to feel his chest on mine.

When I went back into the living room, Rob was looking at my bookcase, his head cocked to one side. There were technology books, literary fiction, and the cozy mysteries that got me through long weekends. I stood and watched him.

"I love to see the books someone reads. It says so much about them." Rob turned and watched me come across the room.

"And what did my little library tell you about me?" I hoped my paranoia didn't show.

"That you are very smart, literate, and serious about your work. Yet when I met you, you were far from pedantic. You were delightful. I'm even more impressed. And, may I say, you look lovely."

"If you keep that up, we may not get to dinner." I relaxed and felt much better. He never saw me when we were at RPI. Then he meets me as an heiress. I wondered whether I could trust him. Was this interest strictly because of GDT?

Yet seeing him now, those doubts went away. I looked into his eyes, and I knew right away. Don't ask me how, but I knew it in my soul.

"I made reservations at the Zola. Do you know it?"

"I know of it. Never been. Can't wait to try it."

"Then your carriage awaits." He had a broad smile, and I swore there was a twinkle in his eye.

He held the door for me, then walked to the driver's side. My heart was beating wildly. He had no idea of the torch I'd carried for him. He hadn't recognized me at that dinner in Seattle. I hoped this wasn't my money being the main attraction. I took a deep breath and told myself, *Give it a try, girl.*

Zola was a fine French bistro. It lived up to its reputation. The wine was paired with the meal. Both were delicious. So was dessert and the ruby crusted port wine that followed. Coffee extended the meal, as neither of us made a move to leave. When the waiter brought the check, then came back to see if we were ready, Rob realized he hadn't yet paid, and the restaurant was empty.

We drove back to my little house slowly. I was aware of the time and the moment when we would be at the front door. I wanted him to come in. I was hoping he did too.

Rob parked in the driveway and walked me to the door. I moved to extract my key from my purse as he bent to kiss me. I kissed him back and lingered. He gathered me into him, and I didn't resist. He finally opened the door, and I took his hand, leading him in.

He sat down, while I went to put on coffee. I set out cups and saucers and turned to get the silverware. He came up behind me and kissed my neck. I stiffened momentarily, then he softly kissed my ear. He didn't move as I turned to face him, my breasts brushing against him. I held his face in my hands and kissed him repeatedly.

The feeling that spread through me was pure emotion. At work, I was considered an intellectual, aloof and distant. It was an impression I unconsciously conveyed. But I was also a warm-blooded woman with dreams and desires, enveloped in the heat of passion. I was possessed by a fire that had begun with a spark in Seattle, simmered over dinner, and was refueled when lingering over dessert and wine. Our hands passed over each other until I grabbed one of his and walked into the bedroom.

He began to take off his shirt, but I pulled it up and removed it for him. He unbuttoned my blouse, and I undid my bra. The remainder of our clothes marked a path to the bed. We learned each other's curves and angles and luxuriated in each other's bodies. With gentility and ardor, we satisfied our hunger and thirst.

When I knew that he was spent, I held him fast. I pressed his head to my breast. The experience, the sensation, was wonderful. He would never know how long I had wanted this moment.

He tilted his head and whispered something I couldn't understand. I caressed his face. He lifted his head once more and whispered again. It was too awkward for me to bend over to hear. We were quiet for a few minutes, lying in each other's arms. He raised his head again and whispered louder. I looked down blissfully at him and smiled. "Yes, it is better than coffee."

CHAPTER
TWENTY

SPENCER GRANADY

I've heard that people thought I had Asperger syndrome. Some thought I was eccentric. Shit, I didn't have enough money to be eccentric. I wasn't smart enough to know who Asperger was. I just thought I was shy. I never went to Rob's office. I was uncomfortable around people in general. Especially people in corner offices. Overall, I tried to keep out of sight.

I found Air Germination offices in the Bremerton National Airport. I knew there was a diner where the pilots hung out. I spent some time there talking to the guy behind the counter, buying a slice of pie, having coffee, and learning about the pilots. Damn fine coffee.

Air Germination was a group of crop dusters from the eastern part of the state. They started showing up a couple of years ago working for some rich gent from Seattle. I opened one of my criminal databases and found that every pilot had a record.

I spent about three hours at the diner making notes and going over what I had learned. A lanky redhead came to the table where I was working.

"Mister, you mind if I join you?" He sat across from me before I was able to answer. "You been asking about the Air Germination crew? Is that so?"

I looked over the table to my new friend. "You mean the counterman? Yeah, I was asking."

"Well, I'm one of the dusters. What can I do for you?" Redhead spoke quietly, with a menacing smile.

"I have a client who told me that one of you fellows was spreading something on her property. Something she didn't want. She asked me to find out what was going on. You know anything about it?" I said.

"Nope. Don't know nothin' about that. You'll need to talk to Dr. Herbert, the boss. I'll tell him you're going to call." He got up and tipped an imaginary hat.

I glared after him. You might say it made me angry. I had another slice of pie and reviewed my notes. Emanuel's client found seed packets being dropped on her property. The photos by her ex-husband showed it was one of the Air Germination planes. Why would they be dropping seeds on private property?

I gathered my notes, paid the tab, and left the diner. My old Fiat started right away as it always did, and I pulled out of the parking lot. I decided not to go directly to the Air Germination offices now. Rather, I drove out to state route three into Bremerton and took the ferry into Seattle. There I picked up I-90 to the Snoqualmie Pass and stayed the night.

Rob's clients lived east of the pass. They were the divorced couple who saw the duster dropping seeds on their property. In the morning, I went to see the house. I saw the grounds covered in bushes, helter-skelter across the two acres surrounding the house. But worse were the huge patches of dead grass and foliage. As I drove along the highway, I saw the same scene in narrow fields until I was past Teanaway, when the fields became larger. These were all unapproachable with tall wire fences surrounding ugly, yellow grasslands and bunches of bushes (apparently healthy) sprouting across what should be pastures. I shot photos all morning.

When I stopped for lunch, I sent the pictures to Rob. It appeared that Herbert was dropping seeds from the air, then somehow poisoning anything else growing in the same field. It made no sense. It was time to visit the reptilian Nolan Herbert at his Bremerton office.

CHAPTER
TWENTY-ONE

NOLAN HERBERT

I was in my Air Germination office when the little guy in the old-fashioned hat came by. My receptionist asked him to wait a few moments. There were crossword puzzles, magazines, a few old aviation magazines, even a couple of Playboys in the pile on the coffee table. They were addressed to me.

This must be the guy my pilot told me about. Short, dressed funny. The receptionist got his attention when she announced, "Dr. Herbert will see you now."

As he entered my private office, the detective doffed his fedora. He had to be a detective. He sure couldn't play one on TV.

I had a Keurig machine on a table to the left, with powdered sweeteners, creams, and coffees on a tray. My desk was clean, a few papers in a neat pile on the side and a few pens in a beer stein. I was sitting behind it, hands spread and flat as if I was about to stand or pounce.

But I didn't stand. I simply pointed to a chair in front of the desk. When Granady put his hat back on, I was deeply offended. He sat down as directed, so he had to look up to make eye contact with me. There were no prefaces or pleasantries. Right to business.

"What can I do for you, Mr. Granady? I understand you've been asking after me."

"Yessir, I have. I'm curious about the dusting that Air Germination's been doing east of the Snoqualmie Pass. You have fields of bushes surrounded by dead grass. Most of it's on the property you've bought, but some are on private property."

"Would you like some coffee, Mr. Granady?"

"Yes, thanks. But I'd also like to know what's going on. Especially on the property that you don't own."

"I hope you like cream and sweetener, Mr. Granady." I passed the cup over to my odd guest and took my seat. "You see, that was a demonstration of an error in air-borne planting. That pilot is no longer with us. It won't happen again.

"My fields are excellent examples of the ability of marijuana seeds, delivered by crop dusters, to develop into adult bushes to grow, despite Grounder being spread on the fields. As you probably know, Grounder is the leading weedkiller and glyphosate in the country. It has some deleterious effects. We're working on that."

Granady sipped on the coffee. He made a face. "What sort of effects, if I may ask?"

"Of course, you can ask me anything. The problem with glyphosate is how strong it is. It kills all the growth it touches. It's a little like the coffee you're drinking now," I said.

"Like the coffee . . . What do you mean? It's bitter, but are you telling me there's glyphosate in it?" Granady got to his feet, his face pale, his hands tremulous.

"Mr. Granady, you're a dead man. I must ask you to leave." I walked to the office door, opened it, and smiled.

The investigator looked at his cup and dropped it as he got up to stagger to the door. As he reached the outer office door, he tripped over the transition strip and fell. His hat was crushed under his face. The receptionist, who had escorted him into my office only moments ago, saw him fall. She rushed to his side and screamed. Granady couldn't hear her shriek.

I rushed out of my office into the waiting area. I asked if 911 had been called and checked for a pulse. The EMTs thought a heart attack was the most probable cause of death. I gave my receptionist the afternoon off. *Clever* was Sixty-four Across.

CHAPTER
TWENTY-TWO

HENRY ATKINSON

I spent the day at *The Seattle Times* going over archival material from 1969. Sadly, it was the only print newspaper left in town. Since 2009, the *Post-Intelligencer* no longer had a print edition, and their archives were only available back to 1986. Carolyn took the day to explore the original flagship Nordstrom's. Her day was more expensive, but I was satisfied with the stories I was able to review. We met at Pike Place for a late lunch, looking out over Elliott Bay.

She arrived late, finding me bent over my yellow legal pad, making notes on Seattle's first Major League Baseball team. She kissed me on the cheek and sat across from me. I gathered my summaries and comments and got them back into my briefcase. My book was becoming Talmudic, an analysis on the commentaries and observations of those who lived there. I had accounts of narratives, anecdotes, and yarns that outnumbered the reality of the forlorn baseball franchise.

Pike Place was busy as always, but I had chosen a place away from flying fish and tourists winding through the world-famous market. I could see by the Nordstrom bags that Carolyn had a productive day. She knew I was doing what I came for by the writing on the legal pad.

"Henry, are we going to call Randall? We haven't seen him since that meeting at our house. It's been years. He's not even on your committee anymore. I thought we ought to call. From what Stan Wight told us, I'd guess that Randall has his hands full right now. It might be a nice break for him if we can get him out of the office for a drink, at least," she said.

I looked at my briefcase and sighed. I agreed to call Randall.

The chairman of the board was gracious as always. He made some time for us that afternoon. We hadn't seen each other since he was recruited to join GDT.

"Henry. Carolyn. I thought you two would never leave the east coast. Welcome. Would you care for something to drink?"

"No thanks, Randall. We do get around sometimes. You forgot I have grandchildren in Texas." I wasn't very comfortable here. It wasn't Randall. I'd known him for years. There was something else.

"Of course, you're right. You two always seemed so comfortable in your little town; I can't picture you traipsing across the country. What brings you to The Emerald City?"

"If you're referring to the capital city of Oz, we made a wrong turn in Kansas. I've started to write a book about the Seattle Pilots. Decided to see the place and get local color. Carolyn came along for the ride. Now she knows far more about the one-year wonder than she wanted," I said.

"When he gets the bills from Nordstrom, he'll understand how much I learned about Seattle." Carolyn laughed but quickly followed up. "You know, we ran into Stan Wight and his wife last night. He was telling us a little about Brad Groes, finding his body, and the forensic signs of murder."

I looked up with a start. I had no idea that Carolyn would say that to Randall. She wanted to be involved in the hunt for Brad Groes's killer. She knew what made a good story.

"You know about that, do you? Did he also tell you about the three suspicious 'heart attacks'? All three occurred after the victim had coffee with Nolan Herbert, our acting CEO. One was my predecessor here at GDT. The next was the chairman of our executive committee.

"Remember Morton Jacoby? He was at your house with Stan Wight when they were interviewing me. One of Mort's partners, a criminal defense attorney, found out another man died of a 'heart attack.' He was a crop duster who worked for Herbert, who just so happens to own a crop-dusting company. Morton tells me that that partner has sent his PI to look into Herbert," Randall said.

"Stan has asked us to look into the death of Brad Groes," Carolyn said. "The autopsy report has been kept under wraps given the sensitivity of the market to any news about Groes."

Huntington leaned back in his chair, hands steepled at his lips. For a moment, there was the proverbial sound of silence. He pushed away from the desk, walked to a bar in the corner, and poured himself a whiskey over ice. Two ice cubes, in a large glass. He drank most of it before he returned to the desk.

"I'm not surprised." He paused, twirling his glass in front of him. "What do you know about GDT?"

"Whatever Stan explained to us and what's in your annual reports," Carolyn explained.

"If we include Brad Groes, that's four dead men. Adding him makes sense since his death triggered these others. Four goddamn dead men, yet Herbert is still the acting CEO. It's been almost five years since Brad's death, so no one outside of the firm is aware of the connection. He must have been confident of getting the board's vote to replace Brad. And that majority keeps him in place, though there are not enough votes to make the title permanent." Huntington was pacing the area behind his desk.

"Randall, calm down. We're not equipped to handle another heart attack," Carolyn chimed in. "Has anyone looked into this voting majority?"

"Mort says that the outside directors make up the majority." Huntington had stopped walking and resumed his seat.

I spoke up. "I think it would pay to have someone look into that voting bloc. It doesn't smell right."

"Are you interested in the job?" Huntington cocked an eye.

"No. It's a curious situation, absolutely. It should be investigated—but I'm just interested in the Pilots."

"Henry, don't give me that. No one was interested in them when they were here. That's why they're in Milwaukee." Huntington leaned forward in his chair.

"You know, I remember a few times when you were unavailable back in New York. Carolyn, they weren't just shopping trips, were they? Rumor has it that you've been head over heels in the investigation business," Randall said.

My discomfort bubbled over. I felt like he and Carolyn had set this up.

"I think I know where you got that information, but it ends here," I said. "We did get involved in a few situations we didn't belong in. We rescued a friend who'd been kidnapped. We investigated another friend's death. Carolyn almost got killed. We're not going to do that any longer. All I want to do is get a better picture of the city and how they reacted to a baseball team, for God's sake. A baseball team."

CHAPTER
TWENTY-THREE

Rob Emanuel

The news of Granady's death reached me in the morning. Spencer only checked in when he had something to report, so there were often long periods when I heard nothing from my friend in the fedora.

I was in court when I got word that he suffered a heart attack while visiting Nolan Herbert. I stood up abruptly, interfering with the prosecution's questioning of a most celebrated embezzler. As I approached the bench, I was stricken with a mixture of sorrow and rage. When I explained that one of my closest staff members had died in odd circumstances, the judge halted the trial for the day over the objections of the assistant prosecuting attorney, who claimed this was one of "Mr. Emanuel's tricks."

I explained to my client that this would give me another day to prepare, and I left the courtroom, leaving my paralegal to tidy up. The police had gone through the papers in Spencer's car and found my name. They called the office to identify the body because they had no family to call. My comfort zone was gone with that one phone call; my well-constructed world shattered.

I'd worked with Spencer since I had been in practice. The little guy had loved being a PI. He considered his hat his uniform, along with a well-worn suit, and an attitude sure to infuriate when he decided to unleash it. He got results for me. I shook my head at the memory. I almost cried.

Another death, another heart attack. On the way back to the office, I called Earl Sedlik, the US attorney. I asked for an appointment as soon as possible. When I returned to the office, I walked over to the corner office catty-corner from mine. It was Mort Jacoby's office.

He was on the phone when I walked in uninvited. With an ugly glare, he started to look up, waving at his intruder to get out. One look at my face and he ended the call as cleanly as he could. "What's wrong? I heard you had to leave court this morning."

"You never met him, but you've heard me talk about my investigator, Spencer Granady? He was found dead yesterday at Herbert's Bremerton Airport office. Cause of death, apparent heart attack.

"That's four heart attacks, Mort. Four dead men after meeting with Herbert. I've set up a meeting with Earl Sedlik. You're GDT's corporate counsel. I thought you should know."

We both stood without speaking until Mort told me to a have a seat. He went to the small bar behind his desk where he poured scotch in two glasses with ice and brought one over to me. He sat next to me as we sipped. It was the good stuff.

"Did Granady have any family?" he asked.

"None that I knew. The police found my name in his papers."

"I'm sorry, Rob. I know how long you've worked with him."

"Yeah, ever since I hung out my shingle. He was a good guy, Mort." I sipped some more. "That's why I'm angry. He never carried a weapon. He just asked questions. He had a great BS detector."

Mort finished his drink. He never sipped when he could swallow. "When are you going to see Sedlik?"

"I'm not sure. His assistant said she'd call me today." I tried to swallow the rest of my drink and grimaced, coughed, and shook my head. "Christ, Mort. How do you do that?"

"When you are a big boy, it'll be easier." He smiled as he stood back up. We shook hands. I gave him the evil eye before I went back to my corner office.

Jacoby must have called Randall Huntington as soon I left the office. He later told me that he needed to let Huntington know about Granady's death after meeting with Nolan Herbert.

"He asked me to come over to his office as soon as I could. 'And to bring Emanuel if he's still there.' That's exactly what he said," Jacoby later said.

He reached me as I was going over my messages, looking for one from the US attorney. "Rob, I just talked to Randall. He wants to see us now. We can take my car." Mort barged into my office, talking a blue streak.

I started to object. I didn't want to see Huntington. I didn't work for him. My senior partner could let him know about Spencer. Instead, he leaned in front of me, gathered the square little notes scattered on my desk, stuffed them in my coat pockets, and pulled me out of the office.

"I told him that Spencer had suffered a fatal heart attack after drinking coffee with Herbert. He said to get you and come to his office. Okay, I made up the part about drinking coffee." Mort was a little hyper. The elevator arrived and swallowed us for the trip to the basement garage.

GDT headquarters was close to the University of Washington, north of downtown. The road was crowded. Almost thirty minutes passed before we could navigate the evening rush. I was angry. I couldn't glance at Jacoby even as we entered Huntington's office.

Huntington pointed at the chairs near the "beverage center." It was a goddamn bar. Over the intercom, we heard, "They're here." Then Huntington pulled two beers from the small refrigerator. There was an open bottle of scotch which he offered to Mort. He gave a Shiner to me, kept the other, and went back around to his desk chair just as a man and a woman entered the office.

Huntington pulled two more chairs to his desk, waved the new guests over, and said, "Mort, you know Henry and Carolyn. Rob, these are friends from back east."

CHAPTER
TWENTY-FOUR

HENRY ATKINSON

I wasn't happy. I'd planned a busman's holiday, studying and writing about baseball. That was the plan until I listened to Rob Emanuel and Mort Jacoby describe Nolan Herbert, adding ugly fact on ugly behavior, drawing a picture of malice, debauchery, and deliberate incompetence. Four, possibly five, deaths attributable to Herbert. Based on the information I now had, I could use some help from my cousin Shelley Garçon.

Shelley and his wife, Marian, are an unusual couple. They're part of the fabric of their hometown, Nashua, New Hampshire. They provide jobs for local college students at their bookstore and a hangout at their coffee shop. Marian graduated from North Carolina with a double major and runs the bookstore. Shelley would rather go fishing but he's in charge of the coffee shop. He was a street kid from Boston who became an entrepreneur of sorts.

He was average height, mildly paunchy, with a slowly receding hairline and no gray hair. He didn't look like anyone. You couldn't pick him out of a crowd. He was invisible. Once he was a hitman. He had an ethical standard all his own. He only accepted contracts on the most corrupt, the people whose immorality contaminated Shelley's universe.

There was never a downtime in his business. But when Marian was kidnapped, he pulled the plug on his career and retired on the dividends. Carolyn and I had just met him when he learned of the abduction. This was family. We helped rescue Marian, and we'd quickly bonded, becoming fast, if unlikely, friends.

The murder of one of the richest men in the country was fodder for reality TV, let alone investigatory journalism. Add to this the deaths of four more victims after having coffee with a corporate executive, albeit over almost five years; it fascinated Carolyn.

All evening, the five of us discussed what we knew, and, more importantly, what we didn't know. Huntington's office became a war room with the detritus of takeaway Chinese food, plastic cups of coffee, empty beer bottles, and paper, lots of paper. Carolyn and I were so far beyond what anyone would consider as investigators that Randall was able to get the attorneys to agree to our participation. I was the only one to hold out, only to see my plans recede into the muck and manure of Nolan Herbert's world.

We took Uber rides to get back to our hotel. Randall arranged for our car to be delivered there the next morning. Then Carolyn and I drove to Bremerton, a sixty-five-mile circuitous route down to Tacoma, passing Boeing Field, then north over the Tacoma Narrows Bridge to the Kitsap peninsula. We passed through Fernwood, which reminded me how old I was. I remembered "Fernwood Tonight," a TV show so old that we swore never to mention it to anyone else. Carolyn assured me that she'd heard about the show from her folks. I wasn't sure if I should believe her or not.

We turned west, then south toward the airport. I drove in toward the terminal and the Air Germination building. We were kept away by yellow police tape and a bevy of police. It appeared that the office was being considered a crime scene. Carolyn walked over to a cop with a clipboard and the requisite grim face. He was standing with his legs slightly apart, guarding the police tape.

"Officer, can you tell me what happened here?" she asked. "We have an appointment with Air Germination to arrange some dusting. Thank God, this doesn't appear to be a crash."

"No, ma'am. No one is allowed past the yellow tape."

I'd walked up and was starting to go under the tape. "We have an appointment with the president of Air Germination. That's the smaller building to the left of the terminal."

"Your wife just told me that. You're still not allowed past the tape, sir. It might be a while before you get to see him. Why don't you call and reschedule?"

I stepped back to use my cell phone. I acted like I was rescheduling my meeting. I could have if I'd had a meeting. I didn't. I didn't have anyone to call, but the cop was watching. While he was watching me babble into the phone, other officers were carrying computers and boxes out of the building that had housed Air Germination.

Carolyn reached over to me, and we walked back to the car together.

Then I realized what the young cop said: "It might be a while before you get to see him. Why don't you call and reschedule?" It just dawned on me. This was where the investigator who worked for Rob Emanuel died.

The airport was a center for private and corporate jet flights. The structures to the left of the field seemed to be offices similar to the small building housing Air Germination. There were numerous rectangular single-story buildings, several of which looked like storage facilities, and two square structures, possibly hangars. They all were full, based on the number of cars filling the spaces around each one. On the right was a collection of older, irregular-looking buildings, with folks lolling about, smoking and talking, the usual activity of the busy little airfield.

There was a diner across the highway. Carolyn and I went in for a late lunch and any information we might gather. The diner was as unpretentious as we expected. The long counter between the booths and the back had display cases of pastries and pies. The variety of coffee was limited to decaf and regular. Creamer came in tiny packets slightly larger than the sugar and pink packets of artificial sweetener. The tabletops were Formica, but they were clean and dry, and the tables didn't wobble. Overall, not too bad.

The man behind the counter came over to take our order. I had regular coffee and apple pie, Carolyn decaf and lemon meringue. Carolyn chuckled and shook her head.

"What's tickled you?"

She looked over to me, laughed again, and whispered, "Do you remember that old joke about the waiter in one of those New York delis? The one about matzoh balls?"

I thought for a moment, grinned, and nodded. "Sir, do you have matzoh balls today? No. I always walk this way." I just shook my head and grinned.

"Can I get you anything else?"

"No. I was just curious if you know anything about the activity over at the airport," I said.

"Only that some guy died of a heart attack yesterday, and the cops are going through that office today with a fine-tooth comb. Really bothers me since he ate here the day before. Pie and coffee, just like you folks."

"Damn, that's too bad. I can't believe anyone will blame you though. Were you two arguing or anything?" I had innocence all over my face.

"Nah, just shooting the bull. He had a lot of questions about a bunch of crop dusters. Hard to imagine anyone work themself up over crop dusting."

Carolyn asked why he was so worked up.

"How the hell would I know, lady? What are you two looking for? Are you from the press or cops or something? These guys are my customers. Leave 'em alone. Leave me alone. Finish your pie and get out. It's on the house."

"Hold on there." I jumped back in. "No need to get angry. We're just curious. You tell us that gent comes in, orders pie and coffee, which is what we ordered, and he dies the next day. Then you're angry because we're curious? I think you've things turned around, friend."

"Why don't you keep the pie, we'll take the coffee to go, and we'll leave." Carolyn had her hand on my arm.

The waiter turned and walked off. He reached under the counter and brought two to-go cups to the table. He left without saying anything else. Carolyn shook her head and stood up. I followed. As we left the diner, I whispered, "I think you're right about the matzoh balls."

CHAPTER
TWENTY-FIVE

Rob Emanuel

I met with the US attorney for the Western District of Washington over lunch. Sedlik was busy all day but worked me in out of professional courtesy and personal curiosity. Criminal attorneys never called prosecutors unless they needed to work a deal. Sedlik knew I didn't operate this way. He was a self-confident bastard if I had to say so.

"Earl, thank you for coming." I was seated already, drinking coffee and reading briefs.

"Rob, I've got to be honest. I'm intrigued. You've never called me before."

"Well, I've never been in this situation. First, I don't represent anyone in this case, but I've got information about a murder. Several murders. That's why I'm here.

"I was approached by one of my partners, Maryann Wilson. She handles domestic affairs, divorces, custody, alimony, and the like. She asked me the law concerning trespassing. It appears that someone was dropping seed pods on her client's property. The ex-husband got a photo of the duster. Later that night, that pilot, a guy named Jack Dalton, crash-landed into Bellingham Bay. The coroner ruled that he died of a heart attack."

"You didn't work your way into my schedule for that. Let me know the rest of the story."

"No, of course not. Give me more credit than that, Earl. I'm getting there. First, the chairman of the board at GDT, Biltong Murworth, died after having coffee with Nolan Herbert, as did Ralph Petersen, the chairman of the executive committee there. My investigator died yesterday. He and Herbert were having coffee at Herbert's office over at the Bremerton airfield. And the pilot, Dalton? He flew for Air Germination, Inc., out of the Bremerton airport as well. In case you don't know, the president of Air Germination is Nolan Herbert.

"That's four deaths related to this guy. Four men who had 'heart attacks' after meeting with Nolan Herbert." The waiter came by with our meals and conversation stopped until he left.

"Rob, I'm impressed. Not convinced, but intrigued." Sedlik spoke in the quiet manner his deputies described him as having when he was serious. It forced the listener to lean in to hear him speak.

"You've managed to persuade yourself that these four deaths are the result of meeting with Mr. Herbert. Granted, this belies coincidence, but it remains supposition. You offer me no proof, nor venture a hypothesis. It's happened over several years. Give me something I can act upon, Rob, not an emotional rant."

We finished lunch in silence. As he rose to leave, the US attorney paused for a moment. "Don't be angry, Rob. You're an excellent lawyer. I often wish you were on my side in court. But you've got to bring me more than what you told me to get an arrest warrant. Call me when you have it. And give my best to Mort Jacoby."

CHAPTER
TWENTY-SIX

Nolan Herbert

As I drove to my office at the Bremerton Airport, I began to think about how much this crop of weed would rake in. Minnesota was widely considered to have one of the most rigid medical marijuana laws in the country, but it was also one of the three states most likely to be next to legalize recreational use of pot. I thought I knew the statutes well, at least as of my time at Minnesota State. I was aware of the momentum toward legalization. I intended to make the most of their desire to get high. There wasn't much else to do in the winter except ice fish.

"Sitting on a stool inside a portable ice shelter, with your rod in a hole in the ice—what a setting for puffing on THC. They really know how to have a good time in Minnesota. Must be that wild Norwegian background."

Jesus, I was talking to myself again. Well, no one else to listen.

I began thinking of advertising hookups with vaping devices. They were smart in Minnesota. Not smart enough to get out of the cold, but pretty damn smart.

I was headed to the office to arrange the transport of the crop. The plan was to bring the stuff in from Duluth. Since it was legal in Canada now, I ought to be able to get it in that way. Minnesota should be a much bigger market than Washington. It was colder there.

As I left the highway and entered the airport, I saw too many cars around the office. Police cars. There were also TV trucks and shiny people holding microphones standing around in front of trucks. Too many cars. I kept driving to the bluff behind the diner, where I pulled up behind some trees.

I was angry, really pissed off. With high-powered binoculars, I watched as the cops went through my offices. I stared as my computers and files were removed. More important were the boxes of 1080 that were taken away.

These cops were bumpkins. They'd never know what it was. I should be OK—but, still, that was my supply being removed. Except for Brad Groes, I'd never used anything but a teaspoon of 1080 in coffee. Worked like a charm. I still had a few of those losers at GDT that I needed to invite for coffee. Randall Huntington and Morton Jacoby for sure. I just needed everything returned to my office.

My office was emptied a little after dark. The cops put up some of that stupid yellow tape and went wherever cops go after dark. I waited a few minutes longer to be sure they weren't coming back, then went down and entered the little restaurant from the front. I loved that I was greeted by name and seated in my favorite booth.

"Want your regular tonight?"

"Nah. Bring me a hamburger instead. Onions, cheese, the works. No salt on the fries though. Not healthy," I said.

"Yeah, I know. Listen, there was a couple asking about you and the dead guy yesterday. I got rid of them."

"That so? Were they cops?"

"Don't know. Could have been press. They bugged me." The waiter wandered back to the kitchen. I stared for a minute. I had never noticed before, but I could swear that he walked funny, like something was in his pants that didn't belong. Weird.

I got myself a beer from the self-serve cooler. I was hungry, and they made a damn good burger. I decided I needed to get laid. I called a few ladies from my contact list. It took a while before I got one who wasn't busy and didn't charge much. Wouldn't be a bad night after all. A burger with an ice-cold beer, then a hot piece of ass.

When I was in town, I spent most of my time at Air Germination. That was my real job now. GDT annoyed the hell out of me. Sure, it paid well and had great benefits, especially great vacations, but they still wouldn't remove "acting" from my title. I showed up for the board meetings, but that was all from me.

However, Air Germination was mine. All of it. I controlled the seeding, the distribution, and the sales of the crop. I needed farmers, of course I did, if they remembered they worked for me.

Granted, there were a few hot shots on the GDT board with MBAs. Who the hell did they think they were? I had a PhD from Minnesota State. I was as smart as any of those ass holes.

To be sure, there were certain things I may have gotten wrong. For example, I thought the Twin Cities was a hotbed of marijuana use. Not true. I lived in Washington State where the sale of recreational pot was legal. Pot sales were much higher here. However, I decided to sell my crop in Minnesota since I'd gone to school there. I was loyal that way. The fact is that only the sale of medical marijuana was lawful in Minnesota. Facts like that didn't bother me. Facts usually got in the way.

After the police left, I hunkered down in my Air Germination office. I'd been preoccupied with getting coffee laced with 1080 to Randall Huntington and Mort Jacoby. The THC crops were being harvested and packaged for the trip to Minnesota. My pilots had been giving me a hard time about that until Jack Dalton had that unlucky accident in Bellingham. Most of them remembered when that farmer had a similar unfortunate episode in the office. They became much easier to work with after some subtle hints like that.

The more I considered the coffee arriving at GDT's executive offices, the more annoyance crept into my head. Who had sent that gumshoe, Granady? The little shit died fast. I realized I never found out who hired him. Damn. I'd have to nose around GDT on my own.

CHAPTER
TWENTY-SEVEN

RACHAL GROES

I was now one of the wealthiest women in the country, something I never talked about. No one at work needed to know. I'd changed, I guessed, subtly I hoped. The changes would be discernable only to the most observant—in other words, other women. My little cottage glowed with a touch of class by the strategic use of paint and some tchotchkes you could find in the towns around Palo Alto. My wardrobe was upgraded to fit my taste. To top it off, I was now the head of the cybersecurity division at work. What with the news of major hacks at some of the largest companies in the country, my team was busier than ever.

Whenever there were questions about the new look of my bungalow, I attributed it to my well-known frugality and recent promotion. I gradually loosened up at the office, which the other women attributed to my boyfriend. They didn't know Rob, but they knew something had changed. They just knew. I had to smile when I overheard them going on about me. I didn't bother to break in except to ask when their next project would be ready.

Rob and I alternated between Seattle and Palo Alto on the weekends. Occasionally I would tie in a meeting with Randall Huntington when we were in Seattle. This past weekend, after Randall and I had gone over the latest figures at GDT, I met Rob at his office. We were going somewhere special. That is, until I saw him.

He was at his desk, tie askew, a Shiner making a ring on the clear glass, a long yellow pad in front of him, full of nonsense. His sleeves were rolled up, the right to the elbow, the left at the wrist. His hair was tousled, showing the effects of running his fingers through it over and over. He looked up as I entered the room, his face grim, not the smile that lit up my world. I went around to the back of the desk and held his face in my hands.

"What's wrong, honey? Are you alright?" I'd never seen him upset. Out of sorts maybe, but not this.

I stood on my toes for a kiss. I held my arm around him as we walked to the couch. After we sat, he turned and began to talk. "You never met my investigator, did you? Spencer Granady. He was an odd ball, always dressed in an old suit, wearing a fedora. Kept away from here. Had his own office. Did good work." He stifled a cry and shook his head.

"Was—is he . . . is he dead?"

"Yeah. He was looking into a guy named Nolan Herbert. He's the acting CEO of your company."

I broke in. "My company?"

"Rachal, it's the company that your cousin was running when he was killed. That's how you inherited all that money and stock. This bastard Herbert is also the president of a crop-dusting company over at Bremerton. Spencer was there when he had a 'heart attack' after having coffee with Herbert.

"He was down there because I sent him. It seems that three other men have had heart attacks after having coffee with Herbert over the past few years. I went to see the US attorney for the Western District of Washington today. He doesn't think I have a case. Four dead men but I have no case." Rob was up pacing. He became quiet and stopped in front of me. "I'm sorry."

He walked over to his desk and picked up his beer, finished it, and sat back in his desk chair.

I hadn't moved while he talked. It was quiet as neither of us spoke until I slowly turned toward him. I was sure that my heart could be heard across the room.

"Do you want me to go? You can be alone." I was terrified of the answer. I didn't want to leave. I wanted him to want me here.

"God, no." Rob stood up and stepped over the beer bottle he'd knocked to the floor. He walked across to me. "I'm sorry. I feel like shit. Please don't go. I've been sitting here since I got back. I didn't accomplish a thing. Sedlik was right. There's no case. It's a terrible story, but it isn't a case. And I don't know what to do about it. I'm sorry."

"You've said that already. I believe you. Now be quiet." I reached up and pulled him in for a kiss. I got no argument this time.

We missed our dinner reservation, but it didn't matter. We got to the Boat Street Kitchen just before closing. It was quiet, a discreet little place for us to have a good meal and talk. It was good to simply talk. Rob was able to unwind. I watched him and listened. He wanted to fix this situation. He wanted to nail Herbert, but it wasn't his case. It wasn't anyone's case. All we could do was talk it through.

We did that. We talked until closing. We shot the bull, talked about our work. When we realized that the restaurant was about to close, we looked at each other and smiled. We went back to Rob's townhouse. It was a good evening after all.

CHAPTER
TWENTY-EIGHT

SHELLEY GARÇON

Many people consider me sophisticated. I'm knowledgeable about wine and thoroughly enjoy drinking it. I love spending time with my wife at home or going fishing with her. We even work together in a bookstore and coffee shop we own.

I was somehow related to Henry Atkinson, though it must be on the other side of the family. While Henry loved baseball lore, I was attracted to the parks and stadiums where the games were played. I'd been to all of them except Sicks' Stadium. When Henry mentioned that he and Carolyn were going to Seattle to research the woeful Pilots, I was immediately attracted to the idea. Sure, I knew the team had moved, but I hoped the stadium was still around. I decided to see Safeco Field, the home of the Seattle Mariners, if old Sicks' was finally torn down.

Alas, the stadium, the home of the Pilots, was no more. It had been replaced by a Lowe's Home Improvement store. Although the location of the bases and pitcher's mound were marked in the store, it was a gimmick, and I hated it. Marian and I made it to Safeco, but I was now in a sour mood.

We caught up with Henry and Carolyn by phone to make plans to meet for breakfast. Henry seemed happier than usual to get together. I had to raise an eyebrow when I heard that. Henry was anxious to get together only when the scent of skullduggery was in the air, usually murder. I loved that word: skullduggery.

My wife and Carolyn had become fast friends ever since Carolyn had gotten Henry and I into the house where Marian was being held by a pair of dirt bags. Carolyn had impersonated an old friend of mine, which allowed us to get in and get Marian out and Henry to eliminate one of the vermin. Ever since then, the ladies have talked on the phone daily. Every day. At least, Henry has the other half of my phone bill.

Henry had been really down before I called. Marian had told me how excited he'd been arriving in Seattle. He was following in the footsteps of the Pilots, even if that meant walking from hardware to plumbing and electrical to get from first to third. The archives of *The Seattle Times* fleshed out the ghosts of the one-year team. Carolyn was scoping out the original Nordstrom's and planning an outing with Marian when we got here. However, when Carolyn became interested in the murder of Brad Groes and the ensuing string of "heart attacks," Henry's mood turned. He simply wasn't ready to join the hunt. Marian told me about their trip to Bremerton. I was dreading meeting up with them. Doom for breakfast.

I suggested we meet at the Portage Bay Café, the Roosevelt location. Henry didn't know how I always knew where to eat, but I was right almost every damn time, so a little before seven, he showed up. Carolyn said she'd be by later. By the time Marian and I arrived, Henry had a table, a cup of coffee, and the newspaper. He had pushed two small tables together, which drew ugly looks from the staff until we arrived. Henry perked up when he saw Marian and seemed to be glad she brought me.

The staff always perked up when they saw Marian. Marian did that to people. A crowd had filled the place and were lined up outside the door by nine. That underscored the popularity of the place with the locals, but today they got to see my wife. The men drooled; the women envied.

On the other hand, I was ebullient when Marian and I sat down. I'd already been to Safeco Field. This was a very human-scaled city. I planned on being a tourist, walking and gawking. Marian planned on shopping. C'est la vie.

Over a very full breakfast, Henry laid out the problem as he saw it. At least four men had heart attacks after having coffee with Nolan Herbert, who had been appointed the acting CEO of this huge company, GDT, after the gazillionaire Brad Groes disappeared.

"You're telling me that the last dead guy was a private investigator? Why aren't the police all over this?" I was incredulous.

"The US attorney thought there wasn't enough to make a case, considering the age of the dead men, the time between the 'heart attacks,' and the lack of a motive. Other than Brad Groes, what did Herbert gain from killing each man, if he did gain anything?" Henry said. He was visibly annoyed. "I can't say I disagree with the attorney, but it does raise suspicions."

"For Chrissakes, Henry, you're a lawyer. You know he's right. If you're going to try to get this guy, you have to think more like me." I was grinning. Hit men didn't grin. It sent a frisson of dread through Henry. I could see it. Marian was used to it.

"Honey, I thought we were here on holiday." Marian wanted to go shopping,

"We are, dear, we are. I was giving Henry some advice, that's all." I paused, then, speaking quietly, I resumed. "These deaths appear random. If this fellow Herbert is who you and the board suspect, you need to be more proactive, but not in his face, like the private dick. Get a GPS tracking device for his car. You can get it from Amazon or Walmart. Find out how he keeps his job. Something smells wrong there. If you think you have to make contact with him, just don't go to that diner. There's more than matzoh balls hanging around."

Carolyn walked over to the table just as I finished talking. She kissed her husband, then Marian and me before she sat in the empty chair.

"So, the princess decided to join us," Henry teased her.

"No, smarty pants, I ate near the hotel. I was finishing up the quarterly reports from GDT. From what we learned at Randall's office the other night, all of the votes keeping Herbert in office come from the outside directors." She turned to us.

"Randall Huntington's the chairman of the board and a friend of Henry's from some conservation work back east. He was interviewed for the job at our house by a law school classmate of Henry's and the corporate lawyer for this GDT company. That's how we got involved."

"Sounds too rich for simple folks like us, don't you think?" Now Marian was smiling, which looked much better on her.

CHAPTER
TWENTY-NINE

ROB EMANUEL

Ever since the merger with BB and BB, I was busier than ever. I had the respect of my peers. I could face down the county prosecutor in court without breaking a sweat. My private life was focused on one beautiful woman. Whenever I thought about her, I became anxious and broke a sweat. I had criminals for clients, hardened and often cruel criminals. That's what I did for a living, but I didn't have the nerve to ask Rachal to marry me.

Nolan Herbert was something else altogether. There were too many heart attacks happening around the do-nothing CEO. He was the cause of these deaths. I knew it. They weren't coincidental. I wanted Herbert off the streets, locked up for the rest of his life.

I never thought that way. Not until Spencer Granady was killed. I knew it wasn't a heart attack, but how could I prove it? Randall introduced me to old friends who were "looking into the deaths," a retired patent attorney and a former journalist. They looked like nice people; they really did. Who the hell wanted "nice people" to find a murderer? Not me.

No, I wanted someone else on Herbert's tail. I had my assistant pull a client list for me. I'd kept most of them out of jail. Maybe I'd get something in return. There was a

Native American, a Yakama, named Sam Watlamont, who looked like the perfect candidate. The poor bastard really was innocent. The cops hadn't believed a word he said. He could be just the man who might be able to give me a hand.

Angie Warren and Sam Watlamont had been living together for almost three years. Their parents didn't approve of an unmarried white woman and a Native American truck driver being together. Things were made worse when he was arrested for breaking and entering, burglary, and assault and battery. Never mind that he was acquitted of all charges. Never mind that someone else was arrested and convicted of the crime. Angie and Sam were not popular with their families.

Angie answered the phone when I called the house. She was home early from work and let me know that she'd have Sam call as soon as he came in. Why was I calling? I could hear the concern in her voice.

Sam drove a truck, a big rig he owned. Most of his jobs took him out of town and were usually four days long. He had just returned from a trip to Modesto, California and had a three-day weekend at home. He wasn't worried about the call from me, but he was curious.

"Mr. Emanuel, how are you? This is Sam Watlamont."

"Sam, thank you for returning my call so soon. I hope I'm not bothering you."

"No, not at all. I was about to kick back and read the paper."

"Good to hear. Sometimes, I think no one reads them any longer. Look, Sam, I need to ask you for help this time. I want somebody followed."

There wasn't much that made Sam hesitate. Certainly not fear; at six feet two inches, he was broad shouldered, considered strapping by the elders and muscular by Angie. Most people just avoided him.

"Sam, you still there?"

"Yeah. Sorry, but you surprised me."

I told him the story. I finished up by assuring the startled truck driver that he would be paid well.

"Mr. Emanuel, I don't want to be ungrateful. You saved my life. God only knows what would have happened to this Yakama in prison. But I don't want to be in a position to be caught doing anything illegal. You want me to snoop around after a CEO of one of the largest companies on the west coast. What if he finds out and calls the cops? Who are they going to believe?

"I can't give it my full attention. I've got a business to run, Mr. Emanuel. I could offer three days at best, between my long hauls. Thanks for thinking of me, but no can do."

"I thought you might say that. I don't blame you. I've been frustrated that there's nothing I can do. You're right, unfortunately, about the cops.

"Forget about it, Sam. Get some rest. Maybe we can get together for dinner. I've got someone I'd like you and Angie to meet. I'll call you."

I hung up and went into the kitchen. I called Rachal to see what she thought about having the Atkinsons over for dinner.

CHAPTER
THIRTY

Shelley Garçon

Henry took my advice to heart. His life as a patent attorney was a distant memory until I mentioned it. He had thought retirement would be pleasant, a relaxed lifestyle with time for his wife and reading. But as it is said, "Man plans, God laughs."

His adorable wife turned out to be wonderfully mischievous, baseball was in the background, and his days were, more often than not, filled with malevolence, misdeeds, and murder. Henry's had to shoot to save my life. He killed a man when we were forced to violence while rescuing Marian from kidnappers. I'll always have his back. I'm along for the ride, bringing advice, a never-ending source of weapons, and my splendid taste in wine and good food. We weren't particularly chummy, but he tolerated my insults and appreciated Marian's insights. I even got along with Carolyn's father much better than he did.

So it was that my second cousin once removed, or whatever we were, and I found ourselves at Walmart, where we picked up the Spy Tec STI-GL300 Mini Portable Real Time GPS Tracker with a two-week battery life and a six-month extended battery pack for fifty bucks. Henry added the Walmart Protection Plan by Allstate. If he was going to spend fifty dollars, he was going to protect the device. I swear I was grinding my teeth when we left the store. So perfectly Henry. He flew to Seattle first class but made sure to get a warranty on a fifty-dollar device.

Marian had found out where Herbert lived by the time we returned. It was on the northwest side of Bainbridge Island. Some of the homes in this area sold for between two and three million dollars—not a bad area at all. After dropping off Henry, we decided to go for a ride to see what could go for that much money. We were East Coast people, from North Carolina to New England. This was a new world for us.

It was dusk when we found the house. Marian parked behind Herbert's car, which I identified by the license plate. I was able to get under the car, attach the GPS tracker, and join my lovely bride on a walk around the neighborhood. It was much darker when we returned to the car.

Standing in front of the house, partially illuminated by the streetlights, was a police officer. I'd noted him walking up to the house. I couldn't make out where he was from, but he was a cop. I could always sense a cop nearby. This one appeared to be a Native American.

We took Route 305 back to Bainbridge, then the Seattle Bainbridge Ferry to the mainland. Marian found on her cell phone that the Port Madison Reservation of the Suquamish Tribe was just across the Agate Passage from Bainbridge Island. The cop may have been a tribal policeman. But why was he there? Marian tried to call Carolyn but couldn't get service from the ferry.

When we couldn't get in touch with Henry, we stayed on the ferry for the return trip back toward the Port Madison reservation. We were the last trip of the day, so they let us turn the car around to exit. It was late when we crossed the Agate Passage Bridge, but Marian found signs to the Casino Resort where we got a room for the night.

It was chance when two Native Americans sat next to us at breakfast. One looked familiar, and the other was wearing a quasi-military uniform. By the time we'd finished our coffee, I recognized the "cop" from last night. "Honey, don't turn now but check out the guy to your right. The one who isn't in uniform. He's the guy who was at Herbert's house last night. Get as good a look as you can."

A few minutes later, as she was having some juice, Marian mouthed, "Got him."

I watched him go to his car as Marian checked out. We trailed (apparently without notice) as Sam drove back down Route 305 to the ferry. We followed him on and parked for the ride. Some of the passengers went to the railing; others went to the passenger section. There was a calm, well-built man, obviously Native American, who got himself a cup of coffee and read the paper. We sat nearby until docking when he drove home. I don't think he ever realized that he was being followed.

"What do you think, hon?" I asked as we stopped at the end of the block. "Somebody asked this guy to check out Herbert. I'm guessing he borrowed the uniform from that security guy at breakfast to pass as a cop. In the dark, it was easy. Christ, we thought he was a cop. The question is, who hired him? And why?"

I got out of the car and pulled a camera with a telephoto lens from my valise in the trunk. I sat in the back of our car and focused on the license plate on the faux cop's car. Marian drove slowly up the street, while I kept snapping pictures. I was aiming for the VIN above the hood at the bottom right of the windshield. Marian kept driving out of the neighborhood.

We made it back to our hotel, where I wrote down the plate number and zoomed in on the VIN. I got it all but one digit. Marian got online. Within ten minutes we had his name and found out he was a truckdriver with his own rig and had been one of Emanuel's clients. The counselor got him off scot-free of all charges. Years ago, my beautiful wife had been gifted LexisNexis by a client, and we continued to use it. Having access to computer-assisted legal research serves its purposes.

When Marian called Carolyn, they were waiting for a call from Rachal Groes. They talked for a bit, and Marian told her what we'd found. It appeared that Rob was so frustrated with Henry at the meeting in Huntington's office that he started to think he needed some muscle to investigate Herbert. Of course, Carolyn knew that many people were frustrated with Henry.

She told Marian that she'd call back later. Marian and I decided to go trolling for stinkfish. We went back to Bainbridge Island. I parked a distance from Herbert's house, where I was still able to watch the house using high-powered binoculars. Marian and I looked for any movement from the front of the McMansion.

When we saw him leave, we turned on the tracker and watched as he went over the Agate Passage Bridge on

Route 305. I walked through a small, lot-sized park and continued to the back of Herbert's house. I quickly attached a hookswitch bypass to the telephone line as it entered the house. At one inch by two, this tiny contraption could pick up any conversation within four hundred square feet. I leisurely walked back to the park where Marian was waiting at the curb.

She'd already called Henry to let him know where Herbert was heading and that the hookswitch had been attached. We had our stinkfish.

CHAPTER
THIRTY-ONE

HENRY ATKINSON

As it were, Carolyn and I were to have dinner with Rob Emanuel and his friend. When I found out that Rob's friend was Rachal Groes, I believed we'd been summoned, not simply invited.

They lived in a two-story town home with underground parking. I mumbled that if Rob could get the lady to marry him, the house would get much larger. Carolyn gave me one of those looks that spoke volumes. I wasn't comfortable at all, but my much-better half was looking forward to dinner. She explained that she was fascinated by the dirty tricks and tactics that had enveloped this company and shrouded at least four deaths over the past five years. Her journalistic background, the ink in her veins, wouldn't allow her to let go of this story.

Rob met us at the door, a Shiner in hand, and brought us into the living room. We exchanged small talk for a while until Rachal entered the room with a tray of vegetables and dips. I stood and Rob kissed her on the cheek. Then he introduced her to us.

"I hope you don't mind, but we're having delivery pizza tonight. It's the best place in town. It's why I bought this house. The pizza parlor is walking distance." They brought us into their dining room where Rachal had set out plates and a large bowl of salad with three bottles of different dressings. As we sat, Rob went to call the delivery service. Rachal pointed to a drink refrigerator in the corner of the room. We were free to serve ourselves. Shiner's, some local brands, and Washington State wines.

I realized this really was informal. I was surprised and chagrined that I had even thought we were being called to be impressed.

After splitting two very good medium pizzas, unending salad, and beer from the bottle, Rob brought up why we were there.

"Sometimes, Rachal gets upset with me because I just want people to know how lucky I got that she'll be seen with me." With that, he ducked as she swung a dish towel at him.

"I asked you both here tonight to talk to you. You know Randall from back east. You went to law school with Stan Wight, and you've met Mort Jacoby. They are all very enthused about having you investigate Nolan Herbert and his involvement in possibly five deaths," Rob began.

"I see a retired patent attorney and a former journalist. Rachal is impressed that you've won Randall's vote; they've worked together.

"My investigator is now one of the dead men. I've got to tell you, I'm frustrated. I even reached out to a former client, Sam Watlamont, but he turned me down. How the hell can you help me get anything on Herbert?" Rob had been pacing. He stopped to take a seat again.

Everyone was quiet. I got up and pulled out another Shiner.

"Rob, I admire how candid you are. You must be hell on wheels in court. Personally, I hated going to court. Still do. I'd rather read and write about baseball most of the time," I said. I went back to my seat.

"Life is a little like baseball. I don't know if you follow the game. Long periods of little activity, just good pitching and excellent defense. Then there's some commotion, usually unexpected. The ball can go through your legs, the outfielder loses the ball in the sun, or overthrows the base. All errors, and you lose the game on unearned runs. It's really shitty.

"Carolyn and I don't like to lose on unearned runs. One of us sees the error, and it gets to us. Sometimes, you just have to see if the pitcher's curve ball is breaking or if his fast ball is always high and outside. Can the catcher make the throw to second? Is the outfield grass too slick? Maybe the batter needs to duck. That's all hooey or twaddle to some people. I know, but that's how we work. We look out for errors, we follow the money, and sometimes we have to duck."

"You're not kidding with all of that are you?" Rob was taken aback. He looked at Rachal and shook his head.

"He's completely serious," Carolyn said. She had just refilled her coffee and Baileys and sat back down.

"I've been looking at the financials for GDT. Haven't any of you worked out why Herbert has kept his position there?" she asked.

"The feeling on the board was that the market value of the company would crash if he was removed. At least that's what Mort Jacoby told me," Rob said. He looked less rattled talking to my wife. I don't think he was into my baseball allegory.

Rachal agreed with him. "Randall told me just that. The market value of the company cratered when it was announced that Brad was missing. Upper levels of the company administration were so rattled by that since then that they're afraid to move."

"Excuse me, that's bullshit. Herbert's had the position of acting CEO for five years now. If anything, the market would react with glee if he was let go. But look at the outside directors. They're solidly behind Herbert. I'm thinking insider information. You know, personnel changes, hiring, firing, retirement. Some problems might merit discussion in the executive committee. Some decisions made in the executive committee will affect corporate performance. Those changes are on the agenda but may never get mentioned in the meeting. Even if they do, Herbert can get the information to his buddies before the meeting. I think Mort, as the corporate attorney, should be checking into any stock moves that are out of the ordinary. Anything that reeks of insider trading. Read the annual reports. Contact the SEC," Carolyn said. She leaned back and sipped her Bailey's.

"You know, you're right. That son of a bitch is buying the votes to keep him there. Do you think they can get rid of him through the SEC?" Rob was back in the fray.

Rachal mixed Kahlua and Baileys in her cup. Sometimes you don't want to add coffee; it might dilute the taste. "Look, the SEC can only prosecute civil proceedings. They have to partner with the FBI or the DOJ for criminal charges, but GDT could get rid of Herbert because of SEC findings. I think I can handle that, but it still doesn't answer the questions raised by the so-called heart attacks," Rachal said. Carolyn looked approvingly at Rachal. She was no silly heiress.

"No, it doesn't," Carolyn said, "and I'd add Brad Groes's death to that total. Henry and I met with Stan Wight after we arrived. We've seen the autopsy report. It was definitely murder."

CHAPTER
THIRTY-TWO

RACHAL GROES

The Atkinsons were an interesting couple. Henry could speak about baseball and life in a philosophical manner. Baseball is life. I guess a double play restores balance to the world.

Then his wife analyzed the misadventures and misbehavior from members of the board of directors that could bring in the SEC. She even suggested that we bring them in. She delivered a hard-nosed report, no frills, nothing philosophical. All in the same conversation.

On the way out, Henry happened to mention that they'll be investigating the deaths associated with Herbert, but, of course, they would accept any professional help we could provide. All with a straight face.

"Look, we would welcome working with a professional, another PI. I have my license, but not in Washington. Anyway, I haven't finished the research for my book, but Carolyn thinks we can help. Stan did ask. That's why we were at that little meeting Randall set up with you and Mort Jacoby. We won't get in your way though. If you want us to leave it alone, just let us know." Henry stood up and gestured to Carolyn.

Rob appeared dumbstruck. I got their coats and walked them to the door. "We'll call you tomorrow, in the morning."

We'd invited Henry and Carolyn to get to know them. Something informal, relaxed, not threatening. What we learned is that those two threw away the mold when they were together. Philosophy, the SEC, private investigations. Good Lord.

"Rob and I had a long talk last night." I reached Carolyn on her cell phone the next morning after Henry was off to meet an old baseball player. "Rob felt terrible after you left. He knows Herbert's a killer, but he no longer has an investigator. The idea that your husband, an intellectual, baseball-loving patent attorney and his tough broad wife would now be in charge of making a case to take to the feds was a hard sell. For Chrissakes, he'd just gotten a lecture on baseball as a metaphor for life."

Carolyn laughed. "Rachal, baseball is Henry's life. He works everything else in when he can. I swear, he thinks I'm his umpire. I don't mind. We've worked out the balls and strikes rather well."

"I can see that. Look, Rob and I are going to Bellingham for a few days. It's a neat town south of the border. I'm going to keep him away from Seattle and let him unwind. If Randall, Mort, and Stan want you two on board, so be it. He's OK with it."

"I'll let Henry know. Before you go, do you or Rob know someone named Sam Watlamont? We think he's a Native American," Carolyn said.

I asked Rob to pick up the phone.

"Morning, Carolyn. Did you ask about Sam Watlamont?"

"Morning, Rob. Yes, I did. He was at Herbert's home last night dressed in some sort of uniform. We're checking it out now."

"You're not kidding, are you? Someone saw Sam at Nolan Herbert's house last night?"

"Henry's cousin and his wife placed a tracker in Herbert's car. That's when they saw your friend. Just wanted to let you know." Carolyn must have known she had him. Rob was still digesting this. "Have a good time in Bellingham, Rob. We'll keep you informed if we find out anything."

Bellingham, Washington is the northernmost city in the United States with a population of nearly one hundred thousand. It's family friendly and wide open with eighty-three bars, breweries, and brewpubs, as well as sixteen marijuana dispensaries. The town was just coming off a high as its breweries had recently won forty-six medals in national and international competition. Yet it has tough rules—it was known that some establishments wouldn't serve national brands like Budweiser, Coors, or Miller.

I'd never been to the city, so Rob and I had planned for a few days there, just south of the Canadian border. I was looking forward to the time off from work and getting Rob away from his practice and the death of Spencer Granady.

Rob was unusually quiet as we drove up Interstate 5. It was only about ninety miles from Rob's townhouse, and the late morning traffic was light. He was still going over the Atkinsons' peculiar approach and the loss of his friend and associate. Before we left for the weekend, he had called Mort Jacoby and let him know where we were headed.

As we neared Bellingham, Rob seemed to unwind a bit. He told stories about his first few forays up here to sample the beers, "purely for research," as he put it. He told me about the hotel where he had reservations—the Hotel Bellwether.

To some, it was dated, but we found that the views of the bay and the San Juan Islands more than made up for any perception of age. We took a short walk around the Squalicum Promenade, a walk made famous by Bella, the hotel's canine concierge. We arrived back in time for dinner at the Lighthouse Bar and Grill, then took our after-dinner drinks outside to watch the sunset, quietly holding hands. The temperature dropped along with the sun, forcing us back inside, and we went upstairs to our room.

As Rob opened the door for me, I saw a bottle of wine and two glasses on a tray on the table in front of the bed. In the center of the tray was a small box.

I stopped where I was and took in a deep, shaky breath. I turned to Rob and began to cry, clinging to him all the while. He held me and stroked my hair. When I'd calmed down enough to extricate myself, he closed the door and led me to the edge of the bed where he made me sit. He got down on one knee and opened the box.

"Rachal . . ." Before he could say anything else, I'd pulled him up, wrapped my arms around him, and kissed him.

I nodded and laughed. I hugged him and kissed him and cried. He kept telling me that everything was okay. I didn't need to cry. He loved me. He was never going anywhere. He was just grateful I nodded.

CHAPTER
THIRTY-THREE

MORTON JACOBY

I spent the morning with Carolyn and Henry. They told me that Rob had agreed to their participation. Carolyn was resolute in her belief that Herbert's support from the outside directors at GDT was because he was the source for insider trading. She had me at "hello," as the expression goes.

Henry had a contact at the SEC. Why would I even question that? He put through the call.

After some pleasantries, Henry got to the point with his contact. "I'm working with a company out in Seattle. Something just doesn't smell right. I'm sitting here with the corporate attorney, Mort Jacoby. Could you talk with him? He can give the straight scoop," Henry said.

He was about to hand the phone to me, but I waved it away and put the phone on speaker.

"Good morning from Seattle. I'm Morton Jacoby, corporate counsel at GDT, Inc. Thank you for your time. We have a major problem with our acting CEO, a man named Nolan Herbert. We've been reviewing our annual reports and quarterly statements. It appears the main reason Herbert has been kept on here has been the almost unanimous support of the outside directors. We believe we can prove this is due to insider trading coming from the CEO. We want the SEC to investigate, with our full cooperation."

"Mr. Jacoby, that's a very serious charge."

"I'm aware of that. That's why we called you. Henry gave you a solid recommendation as being the best man to handle this in Washington," I said.

"Henry almost had me fired, Mr. Jacoby."

"Yes, I know. He also told me that you probably will be fired this time if you don't follow this up. If you'll accept some help, all three of us will be available to you. The man the company suspects of insider trading is also believed to be guilty of murder. As a matter of fact, that's why you're our best asset.

"We're holding a press conference at two o'clock, our time, to announce his departure and our filing a complaint with the SEC."

"Wait one second, Mr. Jacoby. You can't just . . ."

"We can, and we will. Have a nice day." I ended the call and turned to Henry. "Henry, are you sure that man will follow through?"

"Absolutely. Fear is his greatest motivator. I'll call him later."

I hadn't been this enthused since Huntington had come on board as chairman. "I'm calling Randall now to get things started. I want every media outlet in town there."

I stood, shook hands with Henry, and gave Carolyn a kiss on the cheek. After pouring myself another whiskey, I called Randall Huntington. I was back in the game.

CHAPTER
THIRTY-FOUR

NOLAN HERBERT

Jesus Christ, that was close. I would have been eaten alive by that load of cops and press. It must be related to that little guy with the hat.

I made it back to my Bremerton office after 1:00 a.m. I needed to see what those dumb cops did to my stash of 1080. I slept there, which annoyed me, but it was safer. I left early, before the diner opened. I hit the gas and took off, literally. I accelerated, going over a slight rise and coming down with a thud as I came around the back of the airport. Once I was on the highway to Bremerton, I took the ferry to downtown Seattle. The trip to GDT headquarters took very little time. My usual parking spot was taken which pissed me off, goddammit, but not nearly as much as what I learned when I got to the office.

No one looked up as I got off the elevator, but I felt them staring as I strode over to my office. I slowed as I neared the door, which was different. I stared at it for a moment before I realized my name was no longer on the nameplate. I looked at the next door over. My name wasn't there or anywhere else. I turned and shouted, "What kind of stupid joke is this? Whoever did this is fired immediately. Dammit, is that old fart Huntington here?"

The room was quiet while I harangued everyone in the goddamn C-Suite. As I turned back to the door to my office, I was face-to-face with the "old fart."

"Mr. Herbert, you were fired this morning by the board of directors. We are working with the SEC on filing insider trading charges against you. Leave the building at once." Randall Huntington had no fear, certainly not of me. He was angry. "This company will no longer be your plaything. Nolan Herbert Time has run out. Do I make myself clear?"

Two rather large security guards were standing close to me. I could sense their presence.

"This is outrageous. You can't do this to me. I'm the chief executive officer of this company. How dare you speak to me like that? I'll call my attorney."

Randall Huntington, the chairman of the board, smiled. "Gentlemen, please remove this person from the building. He can make whatever calls he'd like from the street."

Without further ado, my arms were grabbed, and I was forcibly guided to the elevator, which had been held open. I'm sure my yelling was audible even after the doors closed.

As Huntington returned to his office, I heard him ask to get Morton Jacoby on the phone.

"Mort, everything went well. Sorry you had to miss it. He was escorted out by security, threatening to call his attorney, the media, and anyone who would take his call."

Lompaol Louie had the distinction of being my attorney, dubious as that may have been. A Korean-Filipino by birth, but of uncertain pedigree, Louie had a legitimate law degree and a small corporate practice until I hired him. He even hired a public relations firm to make sure that the business community knew he was the lawyer for the CEO of Global Development Technology, Inc.

Louie's personal life was a disaster. He was always searching for his biological father and wondering why his birth mother had married him in the first place. Louie was madly in love with a woman named Rita Mae Suey, the best-looking woman he knew, but she refused his attention. She was steadfast in her refusal to ever be Rita Suey Louie. It was one of those situations that led to drink. He drank quite often.

In fact, Louie was an inpatient at an alcohol rehabilitation facility when I tried to contact him. Calls weren't allowed at the locked unit except from family. Louie wasn't in a padded cell. It was a high risk of elopement ward. I probably had a better chance of talking to my attorney had Louie been delusional. No such luck. Just major depression. I headed home.

CHAPTER
THIRTY-FIVE

SHELLEY GARÇON

Outside Herbert's house, I was sitting in our rental car, watching and listening to the transmissions from the house. Herbert was either in bed or drinking. There weren't any voices to be picked up. He had been there for three hours when the last lights went out. That's when I saw movement outside the house.

I stayed where I was. The activity was indistinct, more a subtle shift from dark gray to light black. There was little moonlight.

Like an old black and white movie, the motion seemed to morph into a shadow and then into a man. A familiar figure, one I had seen at the same house. It was time to introduce myself.

The former shadow walked across the front yard, keeping out of the streetlight's penumbra. I slipped out of the car when I first saw the movement on the side of the house. I followed his shadow at first, then cut across the side lawn and met him at the curb.

"Evening, Sam. It is Sam, isn't it?"

The big man stopped and stared. "Who the hell are you, mister? And how do you know who I am?"

"Name is Shelley Garçon. Been asked to check out this guy, Herbert. All I've found is you. No uniform tonight, Sam?"

Sam became quiet. He stared long and hard at me. He must have been trying to figure out how I knew his name. Sam was smart. Big and smart. Owned his own rig and everything that goes with that. He must have guessed by now that I probably saw him in his brother-in-law's uniform. I doubt if he thought I was a cop. No one ever confused me for a cop.

"You seem to have me at a disadvantage, chum. I don't know anything about you. Or why I should be talking to you."

"You've got a point there, Sam. Tell you what. I'll follow you to the hotel where your brother-in-law works, and we'll talk."

I kept close on his tail as we drove to the hotel. He parked and walked into the casino dining room. It was still open, but late enough to not be too crowded. I was pleased that Burt was off tonight. I didn't think I would need another hand.

We walked in a few minutes apart. Sam got a table near the rear, and I joined him as the waiter arrived. We ordered a couple of beers. I ordered a Shiner Bock and explained that my cousin turned me onto it. Damn foreign beers.

"Sam, we're on the same side. My cousin's a friend of Rob Emanuel's. So we're both here to keep an eye on this Herbert creep. I know you're not a cop, despite that uniform you had the other night. And I'm for damn sure not one either.

"Before you ask, I was watching the house when you tried the door in your cop costume. My wife and I decided to stay here instead of driving back to Seattle. Lo and behold, the next morning, you and Burt were sitting at the table behind us.

"My cousin's a retired attorney. He handled patents. He was as dull as that sounds, until he met his wife, who's as sharp as he is not. But they hit it off and have been getting themselves into trouble for years and needing me to get them out of the mess they're in. This time, I'm trying to stay ahead of them, and I run into you," I said.

"Jesus, why should I tell you anything? You don't have any authority here, or anywhere, do you?" Sam was irritated, but he wasn't leaving.

"Well, you're almost right. First, my name's Shelley, not Jesus, but I can see how you might be confused. Second, if we're both trying to nab Herbert, we'll do it better together. You really don't want Cousin Henry to come help."

"Pardon me, Shelley, but do you always talk like this?" Now Sam Watlamont was pissed off.

I sat back and looked at him with that approximation of a smile that drove Henry crazy. Now that made me smile. "Sam, listen to me. We're on the same side. Henry and his wife are trying to get anything they can to put this guy away. I know that you and that lawyer Emanuel are connected as well. We need to get together, you and I, to do the heavy lifting. That's all.

"Henry would rather be writing or chasing Caroline, his wife. But they've helped me and Marian, my wife, a few times, and we kind of work together. So, I'm here for the duration, partner," I said.

"I guess I'll have to trust you. You seem to know more than I do about everything." Sam was visibly shaken by now. I had undermined his confidence. Now I had to rebuild it.

"Pal, why don't you call Emanuel. Go ahead. Ease your mind a bit." I pulled my phone out, which made my new friend sit back in surprise.

"Nothing but my phone, big guy. Relax. Or use yours. Do you have one with you?" Sam had been taken off guard. There wasn't any reason to take advantage of him. I guess my good side doesn't always show through.

Sam shook his head, grumbling. He pulled his phone from his jacket. "We have these too."

He called Rob's number. I heard the attorney answer with alarm. "Sam, you OK? I heard you took me up on my job offer, following Herbert."

"Yeah. I owe you too much not to help, Mr. Emanuel. And yes, I'm OK. I'm sitting with a guy named Shelley something who found me at Herbert's house. Says he's working with someone else named Cousin Henry who's also looking into Herbert. How many people are going to be running into each other here?"

Rob laughed. I couldn't hear anything else the lawyer said. It was getting confusing even to me. Carolyn and Henry were hired to find out more about Nolan Herbert. Marian and I were there to help them. I just recruited Sam, who was working for Rob Emanuel. I needed a spreadsheet.

Sam smiled and shut the phone. He waved the waiter over and asked for a Shiner. Looks like I may have picked up an acolyte.

CHAPTER
THIRTY-SIX

HENRY ATKINSON

W e grabbed lunch on the way back to the hotel. I spent the morning at *The Seattle Times* archive. Carolyn came with me so she could peruse the financial pages for news of GDT since the death of Brad Groes. I asked the waiter to hold off with the menu and just bring the wine for now. I was anxious. I took off my glasses and rubbed my eyes. Carolyn was worried to see me like this. Since I retired, I was usually laid back. I could read or write about baseball for hours or listen to one of those interminable games until the wee hours. It always seemed to make me feel better. But working for Randall and Stanford was wearing me out.

"That was Shelley." I'd just gotten off the phone. "He met a trucker who says he's helping out Rob Emanuel because of how well Emanuel defended him. Shelley ran into him at Herbert's house. They're having a beer and discussing where to go next.

"That's great. Really. Think about it. We're supposed to be digging up as much as we can on Herbert. We have my homicidal cousin following him so you and I can do the leg work to nail the son of a bitch. Now Shelley is drinking with a grateful Native American. No one will believe what we've gotten ourselves into." I downed the wine like it was a beer and waved for the waiter.

"Henry, take it easy, please. Let's at least order something to eat first." Carolyn placed her hand on mine to stop me from reaching for her glass. She asked the server for the menus and told him to bring the wine with the meal. Coffee would do for now.

"You and Shelley have been able to follow Herbert physically and with the technology you two attached to his house and car. We were in good shape until the GPS stopped sending us signals. We knew where he was and where he went," Carolyn said.

"The fact that Sam Watlamont feels appreciative to Rob should be a good thing. We need to figure out how to work with him, honey. He's local. He knows more about this area than we'll ever learn. He can replace the GPS for now. Another set of eyes and ears to keep the bastard in view."

The waiter brought our food: Dungeness crab cakes and Penn cove mussels. Shelley had given Carolyn some advice on local favorites earlier. I tried to order the hot dogs with cream cheese. My loving wife suggested I order that when I dined alone. We didn't always agree.

"I guess you're right about Watlamont. Hell, for all we know, he and Shelley will go fishing before we figure out how to pin those deaths on Herbert." I'd calmed down. A combination of more wine, a very good meal, and Carolyn's steady hand did it.

"Has the US attorney responded to Rob yet? He has to see how unsavory Herbert is." Carolyn wanted to pursue Herbert. She had since we first spoke to Stanford Wight.

"I haven't heard anything yet. Rob and Rachal are still in Bellingham. We'll find out soon enough." I signaled for the waiter again, but this time for coffee.

We went up to our room after lunch. We'd managed to stretch that out to mid-afternoon. The press conference was going on, but neither of us watched. Our room hadn't been touched by the housekeeping staff yet. I sat at the table we used as a desk while Carolyn used the facilities.

I had my long yellow legal pad out making angry doodles when Carolyn came back. She didn't like what she saw. "Henry, what's wrong? Is it Shelley or Marian?" She pulled a chair over and sat by the desk.

"No, they're fine. They're being Shelley and Marian. Shelley's enlisted the man they found over at Herbert's house the other night. They ran into each other at the house where Shelley stopped him. They went back to that lodge or hotel run by a tribe and had a couple of beers together." I paused for a minute. "Shit, I told you that already. Jesus, now I'm repeating myself."

"And how is Marian? Didn't she pull the short straw and monitor Herbert last night?"

"She's great. Well, as great as you can be having to sit up all night and listen to his crap. She had sent a copy of the tape to Shelley by messenger after she got home. That's why she slept in yesterday.

"I'm going to meet with Mort and Randall so they can hear the tape once I get it from Shelley. They're together now for that news conference. Shelley is going to try to get the big guy to continue to follow Herbert. I think we need to get the cops involved," I said.

"Henry, that pseudo-cop has a name. We may not know him, but he has a name. He's called Sam. You know better than that," Carolyn said.

"Yeah, I know, I know. It's just that everything we're doing here is turning to shit. I wanted to write my book. Now we're stepping over bodies, I had to speak to that nitwit at the SEC again, and Herbert is threatening to kill more people. We can't call the police, because the evidence was collected illegally and it's too garbled to be intelligible, at least to me. But, yes, I know who Sam is. By the way, his last name is Watlamont." With that, I left the room.

I was still upset as I walked out of the hotel, turned left and went nowhere in particular. I never got angry with Carolyn. I just did though. I never talked down or patronized people. But I just did. I was short with the hotel staff and annoyed with Randall Huntington and Mort Jacoby.

I walked for quite a while. I wanted to sit down and have a cup of coffee that wasn't Starbucks. I had no idea why. I just did.

I sat and cleared my head by thinking about my book. A book about baseball and America. I loved baseball and how it fit in American culture. Oh, I knew football was more popular, more's the pity, but there was something about the way baseball seasons fit in the seasons of life, or at least they used to.

In 1941, Ted Williams hit over four hundred, which no one has done again since. Joe DiMaggio hit in fifty-six consecutive games, which no one has beaten. In October, the long-lamented Brooklyn Dodgers lost to the Yankees in a World Series made famous when the Dodgers' catcher dropped a third strike and the Yankees rallied for the win. In December, the Japanese attacked Pearl Harbor and the world was changed. I thought like that. I did.

In 1969 they held a music festival in Woodstock and Neil Armstrong walked on the moon. Richard Nixon became the president, and someone died of a peculiar virus later called HIV. I wanted to tell these stories around the team known as the Seattle Pilots which came and went after that singular year.

That was the idea for my book. My book. Instead, my wife uncovered an insider trading scheme, my cousin is following an alleged killer, and I'd turned into a boor.

CHAPTER
THIRTY-SEVEN

ROB EMANUEL

I wouldn't admit it, but Spencer Granady's death weighed on me every day, and I wasn't doing a damn thing about it. My PI had been murdered, yet here I was on an extended holiday. I was ecstatic. No, I was grateful that Rachal had agreed to be my wife. That should have been enough—I was engaged to a brilliant, beautiful woman.

She wanted to stay in Bellingham. She was still glowing from the proposal but was acutely aware of my concern.

"Rob, I need to get back. You know, I still have a job I've got to go back to." She knew she needed to take the situation in hand. She knew I couldn't, as much as I wanted to. I thought I would insult her somehow by wanting to leave.

"I'm sitting at breakfast with one of the wealthiest women in the country, and she wants to go back to work for someone. Honey, you can buy the company." I laughed as I said it, but I knew what she was doing, and I loved her more for it.

We checked out that morning and drove on into Seattle. Rachal had already made reservations for a flight to San Francisco, so we drove straight to Sea-Tac for the flight. Then I drove back to my office. The first thing I did was get in touch with Earl Sedlik.

The US attorney for the Western District of Washington was always busy. It was difficult to get through, but his staff knew me as a resourceful opponent. My name resonated in his office. After the news of Nolan Herbert's dismissal from GDT, Inc., Sedlik had recalled my earlier warnings.

"Rob, thanks for calling. I've wanted to talk to you." So far, the big dogs were after Herbert for financial misdeeds. Even the SEC was after him. But it was my concerns about the deaths of that pilot and the executives from GDT that had Sedlik worried now.

Before I had a chance to answer, Sedlik was setting up a face-to-face meeting with me.

"As long as the press and TV aren't around, I'll be there." Defense attorneys weren't shy, just careful whom they were seen with.

I told Sedlik that I wanted to meet at two thirty, at Roxy's Diner, a New York style deli about three blocks west of a statue of Vladimir Lenin and four blocks from the Fremont cut, named for the first Republican to run for president.

We both ordered Green Eggs and Ham. We split an order of potato latkes. Ah, Seattle.

As expected, the lunch crowd had thinned. Earl and I were animated throughout lunch. We took turns calming each other down.

Sedlik let me know that the SEC had gotten involved after news of Herbert's firing made it back east. My law partner, Mort Jacoby, had called them in to investigate insider trading. Gossip had it that a dolt had been placed in charge, but I wasn't surprised. I was a US Army veteran.

I understood government structure. Set up a brilliant organization, then put a dolt in key positions.

I knew the SEC was one of those bureaucracies. Sedlik confirmed the gossip—the dork oversaw the onsite team. That meant someone specific would have to keep him busy, while the rest of the crew from Washington did their work.

After lunch, I again brought up the unusual deaths associated with Herbert. This time my argument fell on much more receptive ears. Sedlik had been brought up to speed. The reports of insider trading gave substance to the story I told. He now knew that Nolan Herbert was more than the skirt-chasing, tanning bed devotee he appeared to be. The bastard being investigated by the SEC was involved in the deaths of possibly five men. Even a criminal defense attorney wanted him scrutinized as a murderer.

"Rob, I'm referring the case to Ed Abrams. He's an assistant prosecuting attorney for King County. He's been around a long time, and he's good at what he does. Refuses to run for higher office. When I need a special investigation, like this one, a capital case, I bring him in. It's a good move politically to work with the locals, but he's also good at what he does. I'm meeting with him later today. We need evidence that's definitive, something that can stick. But I agree with you. Herbert's dirty," Sedlik said.

CHAPTER
THIRTY-EIGHT

Nolan Herbert

The Seattle *Post-Intelligencer*, or the P-I, folded its print edition of the paper in 2009. Nine years later, it was still a digital newspaper. Like the little engine that could, it puffed along, occasionally breaking a big story. My ouster from GDT, one of the largest employers in Seattle, was the big one. It was front page news, if they had had a front page. *The Seattle Times*, TV and radio news, and the internet followed up.

Everything about me was dissected and discussed. Was my PhD for real, or was I a phony doctor as many employees at GDT alleged? What was I doing at Air Germination, a group of crop dusters, for Chrissakes? The value of my old company soared before my office was emptied, allowing local and regional pundits a field day.

I'd made it a habit to let it be known when I'd returned from my trips to France, or when I was squiring women half my age around town. The fact that their IQs and bra sizes were equal became part of the Nolan Herbert lore. I often spread rumors that I would be buying this or that team, and then swore I wasn't in the market.

Christ, those bastards were having a field day on my account. I needed to get home, to my place on Bainbridge

Island. I never took any of the bimbos there. I kept it quiet. I needed the quiet to think. What the hell had just happened?

My office at Air Germination was surrounded. My job at GDT was gone. It must be Huntington and that damn Jewish lawyer, Jacoby. They did it. Godammit, it must have been them. Everyone else loved me.

I took the Bainbridge Ferry and Route 305 almost to my front door. There wasn't anyone hanging around when I got there, so that damn crowd of vultures probably went to my city apartment, my pied-à-terre. I loved to say that out loud. "Pied-à-terre." My trips to France weren't just for sex, you know. OK, they were for sex.

I poured myself a whiskey and sat looking out at the dark waters of Puget Sound. I was trying to do a crossword puzzle, but I couldn't keep my mind on it. I kept coming back to what had gone so wrong. Things were stable until the shyster joined the board. Huntington said he was needed for some reason.

Shit. I'd have to get some 1080 to get rid of these two guys. That would mean a trip back to Minnesota State, finding out if they were still working with the stuff, and then lifting it without being seen. Yeah, I could do it. I poured the rest of the whiskey and sipped for a while, as I laid out my plans.

I was drunk. I was plastered. I was stewed, sloshed, and blotto. There were two empty bottles of Scotch on the floor. I was also. I opened one eye, then the other, trying to get to focus. I had to get to the john this time. I had to. I would kill my good buddies at GDT later. I would. After I peed.

I'd been up all night, drinking and getting angry. I wasn't confused about what had happened, not anymore. I'd lost my job, and my private company was under siege. The more my inebriated dendrites tried to direct traffic around the hills and valleys of my elegant brain, the more my murderous tendencies came to the fore.

Killing Brad Groes was necessary. He was a young man, and I wasn't going to wait around for him to die a natural death so I could get his job. I had the votes. Groes's death provided the opportunity. So, I grabbed the brass ring—or large rock. When that rock hit his skull and he fell, damn that was cool. Poison was more satisfying because it took more planning, more skill. It was more sophisticated. It was definitely more sophisticated. But watching Groes go into the canyon abyss was the best.

Unless I could get back into the Air Germination office, however, I was going to have to rely on more brutal means. I'd have to get a revolver or a pistol. Never could remember which one was which. I wondered how long it would take for the cops to find out what the cans of 1080 were. Maybe a dumb fucker would put a little finger in to taste it. That would be a riot.

Not far to go now. Almost to the crapper. "Oh, shit. My dress pants."

I lay there, soiled and yelling.

CHAPTER
THIRTY-NINE

MARIAN GARÇON

People thought they knew me. Some saw my looks and disapproved of how I supported myself—an attractive woman with a trace of a southern drawl could make an excellent living. I had been an escort, a very expensive companion. I was a hooker. Earning two degrees at UNC bought me my leisure time at MIT's library.

Nobody's thought of me as a prude, not since I beat the shit out of that prick Wayne Borders in middle school for calling me a prude, not by a long shot. Yet I was repulsed by Nolan Herbert.

It was my turn to eavesdrop. I'd drawn the short straw and had to listen to the twit. I didn't like it, but I accepted it. His drunken rambling and his violent outbursts punctuated by vomiting made for a very long night. So much of it was incoherent gibberish, but there was something of note. Herbert was planning to kill again.

Shelley didn't handle it well. He was coming to understand what a sleaze Herbert was. He wanted to call Rachal Groes at her office in California about something to eavesdrop on the go, something portable. She didn't seem to be receptive to the idea. Maybe it was his presentation. She also didn't know Shelley.

He wanted to get this guy. Herbert was just the sort of target he used to specialize in: dishonest, unpleasant, contemptible. Just the thought of it made him feel better. Nobody would miss the loathsome putz. Well, Henry might. He was that type of guy, except when he was defending the family. Turns out he's a good shot.

I'd be upset as well. Shelley had promised me that he was retired from the old life. Except for fishing and the occasional trip to see an old ballpark, the world saw him as a shop owner from Nashua, New Hampshire. We really did own a coffee shop and a bookstore in Nashua. He even liked that life. It was infrequent that he missed those bad old days. Henry and Carolyn kept him busy enough.

The four of us were getting together for dinner that evening, bringing each other up to date on what was going on. Henry, the baseball historian, was scribbling furiously on his yellow legal pad while waiting for his wife and me. It wasn't earned runs or batting averages filling the pages, but notes on a particular kind of varmint found on the streets of Seattle, the home of Skid Road. The satellite readings from the GPS that Shelley had attached to Herbert's car were filling the page in front of him.

The former acting CEO had gone to Bremerton Airport where he stayed the night. He left early in the morning, but then the image simply disappeared from the screen. Herbert couldn't have found the device and stopped to remove it. The car had been moving. Somehow, the damn thing had stopped working. If it had simply fallen off it would still be transmitting.

Henry was already in a foul mood when he sat down at the table. He'd spent the afternoon with the investigators from the SEC. It was apparent that the team was competent. They were aware that the team leader was an example of bureaucracy run amok. Mort Jacoby and Randall Huntington painted a complete picture of Nolan Herbert for the SEC staff and let them have access to whatever files they didn't already have. As the SEC contact, Henry had to occupy the team leader.

That morning, I had slept in. I spoke to Shelly before Carolyn and I went shopping. I filled him in on the information I'd obtained from the overnight eavesdropping. As expected, Shelly was furious that I had to sit through the rants and drunken raves I was subjected to all night. I gently reminded him that I'd heard it all before. He was planning to let Henry know about Sam Watlamont, who felt he owed Emanuel for defending him. He was eager to help around his trucking schedule.

After shopping with Carolyn, it was more likely that Shelley and Henry were the ones out of the loop. As usual, we talked and shopped, shopped and talked. I don't think men understand the difference between shopping and buying something. It's so sad.

Even when it came to fishing, Henry and my husband couldn't quite get on the same page. They both said they liked fishing but Henry's idea of catching a fish must have come from Pike Place Market, where people threw fish to each other.

Over time, Shelley had developed excellent taste, a quality sorely lacking in his cousin. Henry was book smart;

his street smarts were limited to addresses. Restaurants, wines, and overall sophistication were outside Henry's brief. Excluding Carolyn, that is. How he pulled that off remained a mystery to Shelley and me.

We just took it for granted that we were picking the restaurant and decided on Japanese for dinner. A couple of phone calls and a few questions later, we had reservations. Nolan Herbert wasn't on the menu, but he was on the damn agenda.

Supper was excellent. However, the conversation was all business. Shelley was appalled when he heard that Herbert had dropped off the GPS scan screen. Henry was convinced that Shelly blamed him, which wasn't the case.

By the time we split up to go back to our rooms, Shelley and Henry weren't speaking, a relief to Carolyn and me. The missing GPS had driven a wedge between the two men.

Both men swore they were leaving in the morning. Shelley was going fishing, and Henry was going to finish his book.

"Don't check out yet, Shelley. I think I'll be staying for a bit longer." I stood and smoothed my skirt.

"I think I'll stay as well. There's simply too much left to do here. How about breakfast at our hotel tomorrow, Marian? They serve until ten," Carolyn said and smiled at me.

Henry had almost made it out of the dining room when he realized we were still at the table. He came back as we were going over our notes. We were going to work together. Safer that way.

"Carolyn, are you kidding? You're planning to stay?"

"No, I'm not kidding. This is much too serious to leave over hurt feelings."

Henry was simmering. He seemed a little embarrassed, but seriously annoyed.

Shelley was standing by himself. He wasn't nearly as annoyed as he was embarrassed. He said I had that effect on him, especially in front of the Atkinsons.

They were quiet as they left. They knew they'd be getting together at breakfast.

CHAPTER
FORTY

RACHAL GROES

The flight to San Francisco was a little over two hours. The walk to baggage pickup and then to my car took another thirty minutes. Finally, I was on the road back to Palo Alto. I'd left Bellingham early in the morning, and this was the last leg. I was tired, which always made me wonder. I didn't even drive to Seattle; Rob did. I didn't fly the plane; I only read a book. I didn't even cross a time zone. Just the same, I was looking forward to a bath and going to bed.

I kept playing with the new ring on my finger, and it made me smile. Rob had asked me to marry him and gave the goofiest grin when I said yes. It was almost a week, and I could remember every word we said to each other. I always would.

Rob was relieved when I suggested we get on home. It was more than restlessness that I saw in him. He was working hard to contain his agitation about Spencer. He may have been in love with me, but he had worked with the little man for much longer than he knew me. He had to deal with the PI's death. I'd made the right decision.

The next morning, it was breakfast as usual. I was in my regular seat. I didn't have to feign a headache when the regulars noticed my ring and the glow that followed me.

Whatever doubts the staff had about me had long since vanished when I began to spend so much time in Seattle. The ring just made them think I was crazy. I was still in Palo Alto. The ladies who lunched and solved the office social problems couldn't believe it. They were desperate to see a picture of him, at least of us together.

Within minutes of my appearance at breakfast, the news of my engagement and the descriptions of my ring had been texted and emailed throughout the office. I'd guessed I wouldn't get much done; still, I overestimated my work productivity. Then I got a call from Seattle that wasn't from Rob. It was someone named Shelley who said he was Henry Atkinson's cousin.

"Hello. I've only recently met Henry. I'm afraid I've never heard of you. What did you say your last name is?" I asked.

"I didn't say, but it's Garçon. Please call me Shelley. Only the police call me by my last name. I was hoping you could help me."

I repeated to myself, "only the police call me by my last name." What in the world was that about?

"How is that, Mr. Garçon? What can I do for you?"

"Henry and I are working on a case which requires eavesdropping, I'm afraid. I have a GPS placed under the perp's car and a hook switch bypass for his house. I need something portable or mobile that will be similar to the bypass. My source says that you can handle this."

"Mr. Garçon, I don't know who you've been talking to, or how you got our name, but we don't get involved with anything illegal," I informed him.

"Ms. Groes, I've already told you more than I tell anyone about my work. I admire your honesty and your attempt to stay on what you think is the right side of the law. I'm concerned for you that you should ever confuse the two."

Neither of us said anything for a few seconds, a silence that seemed to go on. I was fascinated in a dreadful way, but I finally ended the call, polite as always and strangely intrigued.

What an odd phone call. A group of people working in "secret" to ensnare Nolan Herbert. Henry, Rob, Sam, Henry's cousin Shelley, and now me. Apparently, Sam Watlamont had assured him that I would take the job. He'd been convinced in turn by Rob, who was, after all, his attorney and his boss in this caper. Did Mort Jacoby or Randall Huntington also know what was going on? Would this turn out to be a case of too many cooks in the kitchen or the children's game "telephone"?

I tried to put the bizarre conversation with Shelley behind me but wasn't successful, as I returned to it whenever I thought of Henry and his wife. They were working on catching Nolan Herbert, right? Then I hear from Henry's cousin who tells me to be careful not to confuse honesty with law enforcement. Only the police use his last name. What had Rob gotten himself into?

Shelley didn't even ask for software. I worked for a software company, after all. Somehow, he knew I could get what they needed. How the hell did he know that?

Rob usually called after work. I was pacing the house waiting for the phone to ring. We talked for a long time, about love, work, and the phone call from Shelley. Rob was furious when I told him of the call.

"Did he say that Henry gave him your name? He's Henry cousin, so yeah, that's probably it. I'm going to talk to Stan Wight and Mort. We've got to get rid of them."

"Rob, hold on a minute. He was odd, to be sure, but he seemed to know technology. His comments about eavesdropping were on the money. He was quite complimentary of me. It's just the strange things he said that imply he's some sort of crook or something.

"And what about Herbert? He's been cheating for years to keep his title. If Henry and his strange cousin are getting closer to getting him, I'm not so sure you should get rid of him. Earl Sedlik hasn't been able to help, has he?" I asked.

"He's assigning someone from the King County prosecutors office to the case, someone he values. The problem Earl has is that he's pledged to follow the law and then go to court against a reprobate like me."

"Honey, you're only a reprobate sometimes. I'm not sure your clients even know what that is. Shelley, well, I'm of the impression that he knows."

Rob laughed at that, but he started to use his "lecture the jury" voice. "So, you want to leave everything as is? Even after this phone call?"

"Since I spoke with Shelley, I wanted us to get away from the cousins, their prey, everything. But now, after talking to you, I'm convinced we need to let them do their thing until they either find Herbert or get enough to turn over to the county prosecutor or his investigator. You seem to think highly of Sedlik. I do too. He seems to be on board.

"Rob, honey. GDT has a real problem, even after firing Herbert. This insider trading charge has brought in SEC heavyweights. I know Mort said GDT called them in. Think about it. When a husband calls in his wife's death, who's the first suspect? The husband. Do you think the SEC will be any different? I think you need to use the cousins. They sure as hell are peculiar, but that may be their strength. Unless Abrams has something he's not sharing with you, he'll welcome the help."

"Rachal, I'm glad you're on my side."

"Was that ever in question?" I was smiling.

"Oh, you know what I meant." The conversation veered to a series of compliments and endearments in the language of warmth and love. He wasn't a lawyer, I wasn't a technology specialist, we were just a man and a woman.

CHAPTER
FORTY-ONE

NOLAN HERBERT

My head was pounding, and my eyes were bloodshot. I'd cleaned up fairly well. A clean shirt, a suit fresh from the cleaners, and my new loafers with the tassels. The old shoes were in the trash bin, unwearable. I placed everything else that I'd been wearing in two plastic trash bags that I intended to drop off at the cleaners. If I could get to the cleaners or anywhere else. I was mixing up V-8 juice, Worcestershire sauce, a raw egg, and coffee, trying to remember exactly what was needed to cure a hangover. The pounding was so severe, I couldn't hear myself think.

There were little questions that I had about the repulsive cocktail in front of me. Was it tomato juice or V-8? Was it Worcestershire or Heinz 57? Did the coffee have to be decaf? Why did my fraternity brothers insist on brown eggs? Too late now. I decided to drink it all at once.

When I woke up later that day, I couldn't recall how long I had puked. I was on my stomach, completely naked. I wished I was dead.

Although there were others who felt unkindly to me, they weren't that way to my face until that ugly scene at GDT. Some people said I was overconfident, arrogant, and supercilious, even if I didn't know what that meant. I attributed my success with women to my looks and gift for gab. The money I flashed may have helped a little, I guess.

Spreading cash around never hurt. Not with getting laid or being elected to my position at Global Development, albeit after meeting Groes on the hiking trail. Christ, I almost killed myself on that fucking trail. Hearing Groes fall made it all worth it.

After a few more hours, I staggered back to the bathroom, showered, and dressed once again. I did have to polish the loafers, but it was worth it. There was something about tassels.

It was dark before I felt well enough to drive. I hoped that would give me enough cover to get into my Air Germination office. Those vultures from the press should be gone by this time. The trip was almost thirty miles. At night, there wasn't any traffic, and I got there a little after midnight. The buildings were gloomy, with a rare light scattered across the asphalt runway.

My office was wrapped in an ominous shroud, almost invisible. Good, no one else would be there.

I killed the car lights and found the old wooden building more by habit than vision. There wasn't another car anywhere nearby. I parked on the darkest side and took my briefcase with me. As soon as I opened the back door, I saw the damage. I had no idea how many people had been here, but it had been too many. The rooms were a disaster of paper, empty shelves, drawers strewn about, and furniture turned on end.

I went straight for the closet where I stored the cans of 1080. They appeared to be untouched. I'd forgotten how many were still there. Well, if those damn cops broke into one, it'll be one less shamus to worry about.

I sat in the big chair at my desk, in the dark. I rubbed my eyes, glad that I couldn't see them. A headache was coming on again, but not from drinking. I sat there as the throbbing began in earnest. What the hell had happened to me? One day I was the CEO of GDT, the next I was out. The SEC was on my back. They had done that also, the bastards at GDT.

I thought I had eliminated the big dogs, the Rottweilers and bull mastiffs on the ninth floor. There were new ones up there now. They'd outmaneuvered me, but not for long. I'd be back. I'd destroy them all, and I'd be back.

I fell asleep in the office. I was sore and achy from sleeping in the chair, but I wasn't sick any longer. My head was clear. I knew what I needed to do. I was going to kill Huntington and Jacoby. I wasn't quite sure how I'd get to them, but I was looking forward to it. Especially Jacoby.

The sky was lightening up. I had to get out of there ASAP. I loved those funny little words, the ones people made up out of letters when they were too lazy to write real words. "ASAP. ASAP." I might write a song one day with words like ASAP or SNAFU. I backed into a trash can while I was humming my new song.

Shit. Shit. Shit. I'd made enough noise to raise the dead. I pounded the steering wheel, then slammed the gas pedal hard. The wheels responded in a noisy showering of gravel over every structure within twenty feet. Lights began to go on across the road and behind me. I took a sharp turn from the driveway, the car listing onto two wheels for a moment. I jerked the steering wheel back to the left and tried to brake but came back down on the accelerator. The car almost elevated and came back down with a loud thud. I briefly lost control as I careened forward. The entire airport seemed to be awake as lights came on in my wake back to the highway.

Had there been any traffic, I couldn't have stopped. I was going too fast, my right foot glued to the floorboard. Any possible connection of my brain to the muscles of that particular foot was gone, overwhelmed by the "fright and flight" response of hyper-acute stress—I was scared shitless.

I disappeared. I had to. The SEC was looking for me, even though the inquiry had been kept private after the announcement at corporate headquarters. They always were. Once completed, the Enforcement Division formally recommended that civil actions be taken in federal court against me. They had turned over the information for criminal prosecution to Earl Sedlik, the US attorney. He brought in the FBI to assist with the search. I was in the wind.

I had liquidated Air Germination without fanfare. The receptionist, the weatherman, the pilots, and the vendors received checks and notices that these were final. There wasn't a return address, and the bank account was closed when the last check cleared. The building at Bremerton National Airport seemed to become shabby and rundown within weeks of being abandoned. The managers of the field couldn't reach me and filed suit to have the building kept up or sell it. Occasionally, a dark gray undistinguished car would park across from the remains of Air Germination. The driver never got out of the car. He usually left after thirty to forty-five minutes.

CHAPTER
FORTY-TWO

RACHAL GROES

I finished up the cybersecurity project. The company was happy with the product. They set up a sales division strictly to handle it. I was free to move to Seattle. Rob and I had been engaged for a year. It was time I began to work on a wedding. Of course, Rob was there. GDT was there, and as the largest shareholder, I knew it was important to be available to the board. Did I mention that Rob was there?

I was able to sell my bungalow in Palo Alto without any trouble and at a significant profit. One of my bosses had fallen in love with the place when I had an office party there. As soon as I gave notice, he made an offer on the place, which I accepted. Moving didn't take as long as I had feared. I hired good movers and paid my co-workers to oversee the move.

The relocation was bittersweet, but I was relieved to be in Seattle. I moved into Rob's townhouse and realized that the fraternity house interior design needed a full overhaul. Rob wasn't sure why—that, of course, was the reason it looked that way.

He was delighted that I had moved in. Nolan Herbert had been missing for months. Our concern about him had abated over time. The probes and queries into his disappearance weren't exactly on a back burner but had slipped from the public eye. Even the cousins who had been looking for Herbert had gone back east.

We often mentioned them. The retired attorney who was a baseball historian and his cousin, the hitman. I was shocked but not surprised to find out about Shelley's past. I once read that, "The past is another country. They do things differently there." Shelley demonstrated that for me.

Taking me around the Queen City, as it was formerly known, rekindled Rob's love for the city and seemed to revive his enthusiasm to wake up in the morning. Every weekend we went somewhere new or tried to find someplace that was new once more.

I'd been working hard to turn Rob's condo into a home, a place adults could enjoy. Rob did notice the changes. It dawned on him that his taste had been puerile at best, but more likely worse. He decided to surprise me with a weekend in Bellingham. We hadn't been back to Bellingham since we got engaged.

Rob told his office to hold everything except for emergencies for the next week. We returned to the same hotel, the Bellwether. Again, we were greeted by the gatekeeper, a dog named Bella, and we settled in for the week. We took long walks, tried a new beer with every meal, and made love. Beer with breakfast was a hoot. Having sex was better.

The fourth day we were there, Rob got a call from the office. The grand jury had indicted one of his clients on charges of child pornography, child trafficking, and solicitation for murder. Rob had gotten him off prior charges of embezzlement and income tax evasion. As far as Rob was concerned, this guy could get another lawyer, but the judge in the case had set up a hearing with an attorney from Earl Sedlik's office. Being on holiday wouldn't cut it in his court, so Rob was on his way back before lunch.

We agreed that I would stay since he thought he could be back the next day. There was time for a little lovemaking in the morning, so all was not lost. I spent the day sitting on a balcony overlooking the marina. I read a little, had lunch in the room, and took a walk around the grounds. I was by myself for the first time since I'd moved to Seattle. I was making plans for the townhouse and thinking about setting a date for our wedding. I noticed that a dark gray, nondescript car, which had looked out of place in such a lovely spot, was no longer there. It had been parked along-side the path from the restaurant to the putting green.

CHAPTER
FORTY-THREE

HENRY ATKINSON

During our visit to Seattle, I'd met an elderly Seattle Pilots ballplayer who had been lured back to the city for retirement. He was an ongoing source of tales from the one-year wonders of the west division of the American League. As can be a problem when stories come from a septuagenarian known more for his yarns than his baseball prowess, I had to do a great deal of fact-checking. I found 50 percent fact, 25 percent invention, and 45 percent figments of an overdone imagination. I knew this was more than 100 percent, but the damn whoppers were good ones, and the rumors and gossip had long since passed into legend.

Carolyn and I decided to fly out to Seattle to check some of the more far-fetched tales. I'd check in with Mort Jacoby and Randall Huntington. I hated to admit it, but I missed them a little. Just a little.

Carolyn called Marian to let her know where we'd be. They had married these two cousins, Shelley and me, and had become much closer than friends. No one answered. Probably fishing.

I spent the day tracking down the old Pilot who lived on the generosity of others, the denizens of lounges and bars. He was a gentle soul who prided himself on once being a major league baseball player. His stories about players who had become household names were eagerly sought out—case in point, my cross-country trek to nail down these anecdotes. But daily visits to purveyors of booze and his desire to accept drinks in exchange for a little war story had marinated his gray matter. By the time I made contact, the old man's speech was thick, his breath was flammable, and his stories hilarious, though their veracity was in inverse relation to their length.

I took a cab to meet Carolyn after taking my inebriated colleague back to his room. I had taped our conversation and would start to transcribe what was usable when Carolyn was out tomorrow. I was going to use what I could, but only as hearsay.

After paying the driver and reminding myself once more to start taking Uber or Lyft, I went into a lovely little bistro. I hesitated for a second when I saw Carolyn and Marian sitting together at the bar. They looked up as I walked over and smiled.

"Surprise. Look who I ran into today. Shelley will be along in about a half-hour." She leaned over to kiss me, though she made a face.

"Have you been drinking already?"

"No, but my contact's an old alcoholic and I didn't even find him until he was two sheets to the wind. I took him home in the taxi that brought me here."

"Henry, isn't it 'three sheets to the wind'?" Marian knew those things.

"He wasn't when I got there, but he sure was when we left."

A table had opened up, and we were being seated just as Shelley arrived. Carolyn was delighted, but I was trying to control my irritation. Ordinarily, we had each other's backs, but today it annoyed me to see my cousin there. Not Marian, though. I liked her.

"So, are you here for Nolan Herbert or that book on the Pilots? You still working on that?" Shelley was ebullient. The appetizers were being distributed. I'd lost my appetite.

"You know why they didn't make it? It was the stadium. Sicks' Stadium. No one could get Sick to change the name. It was a bad omen. It wasn't like saying, 'Hey, wanna go to Yankee Stadium? The Red Sox are in town.' Try 'Wanna go to Sicks'? The Red Sox . . .'"

"I know, Shelley, I know. It was also because they weren't very good, and most people had other things to do. Look around, Shelley. This city is gorgeous. The Mariners . . ."

"Henry, be quiet. There's a cop watching us. Don't turn around," Shelley said.

"Are you sure?"

"Are you kidding?" Shelley could always spot a gendarme in the area.

We continued to talk but kept it at a lower pitch. Any aggravation with Shelley was gone. The four of us were hyperalert. Marian had the best sightline to the cop.

"I think we've seen him before, but this is random. He doesn't look like he's noticed us. He may be here to eat," Marian said.

"Marian, sweetie, you know I don't believe in coincidences. Is he alone?" I never believed in coincidences.

"Yeah. I know. He's leaving now."

"Honey, can you tell if he was eating?" Shelley was always suspicious.

Marian had dropped her eyes as she reached for the tartar sauce. "Can't tell. The table might have been cleared before we picked him up."

The cop never looked their way as he left.

"I've never seen him before, have you, Henry?" Carolyn asked. I shook my head.

"Can either of you remember if you saw him when you were at the bar? Do you think he was here first?" Shelley was speaking in a whisper. He was on edge. He was a very confident man, but he didn't like surprises, not at all.

"Shell, I'm not sure. Carolyn and I were planning where we were going tomorrow when Henry came in. I wasn't even thinking about anyone we might have met or known from before." Marian looked from her husband to Carolyn.

"Marian's right, Shelley. We were lost to the crowd until Henry showed up."

I had gone quiet. I'd picked up on Shelley's concern as soon as Shelley cut me off. We were like that. Carolyn and Marian agreed—it was something genetic.

The waiter had brought the entrees and refreshed our drinks. After he left, I asked, "So, what brings you two here now?"

Shelley spoke up now that the cop was gone. "I was hoping to hear from Sam. He was working on the side for the attorney, Emanuel. We'd kept in touch for a while. Then nothing. I called his brother-in-law. He works at the hotel across the Agate Passage from Bainbridge Island.

"He told me that Sam has been overwhelmed with his truck business. You remember he owns a big rig. I finally got a message to him through his girlfriend. She confirmed that he's been very busy, but she got him to call back, and he agreed to meet with me today."

"Why didn't you call him or text him?" I couldn't understand the need to fly from Boston, cross country, to have what amounted to a phone conversation.

Carolyn cocked her head at me. "Henry, why didn't you call or text that old catcher for the Pilots?"

"For the same damn reason Shelley came to see Sam." I knew she was right.

"Sometimes you have to be face to face. Right, Henry?" Shelley was calm, but his eyes were scanning the room.

"Anyway, Sam confirmed how busy he's been, but he told me he's been using his spare time to look for Herbert. He hasn't even told Emanuel. I could tell from talking to Angie, the girlfriend, that she understands, but she's not very happy. She misses him. Unfortunately, nobody's been able to pick up a whiff of the little shit.

"I did get something interesting," Shelley continued. "Remember the morning Herbert disappeared? Just before sunrise, it sounded like a car or truck had run into some garbage cans. Made enough noise to wake the dead. Then the driver tried to peel rubber as he bolted out of there. Sam found debris that looked like a smashed GPS. I think the GPS fell off, and he drove over it on the way out."

"Have the police or feds picked up any trace of him?" Carolyn asked.

Shelley looked at his wife, then Carolyn and me. "There hasn't even been a hint of him. If he's dead, no one knows where the body is. If he's still alive, he's smarter than everyone gave him credit for. The bastard's as good as gone."

CHAPTER
FORTY-FOUR

Nolan Herbert

This evening I was having a meal of canned pasta, canned French-cut string beans, and canned tomato sauce, simmered together, in a small apartment in Tacoma. My ability to elude the authorities had baffled even me. I was hiding in plain sight. Those morons were blind. I had to admit that it was tough living in this shit-eating efficiency apartment, but I couldn't return to my home on Bainbridge Island. They were monitoring my mail and got the fucking bank to freeze my automatic withdrawals. Then the bank foreclosed on me.

I had had the wherewithal to set up a dummy account as soon as I got out of the Bremerton Airport. I had closed the Air Germination office and laid off the crew the same day. Wasn't happy about that, but it had to be done. I had to shut off anything that might lead back to me. I took a risk when I got a post office box. That's when I realized that my beard and glasses were all the disguise I needed. I had to remember my new name, but I pulled it off without a hitch.

Acquiring the gun was trickier. Hanging around bars long enough, you get to know some of the other patrons. Most of the men on their own wanted to keep it that way, but some opened up if you bought them a drink. Ultimately, I found the right guy who sold me a Glock. My new friend might still be with us if he hadn't asked about a gun license. It was good we could share a cup of coffee one morning to discuss it.

I spent hours by myself in my apartment, doing crossword puzzles and plotting my comeback. Going out was simply too dangerous. Even a local cop could get lucky and recognize me. I couldn't afford to reach out to any of the floozies I had escorted around town. Their penchant for talking was up there with their talents in bed. I missed them.

The SEC investigators had turned my case over to Sedlik once they determined that there were indeed grounds for criminal charges. They only prosecuted civil cases themselves; criminal cases were referred to the US attorney's office. So now I had the feds on my tail, but at least that PI with the stupid name was no longer around to get in the way. What the hell was his name? It was something like Grumpy or Cranky. No, that was his last name. How could his mother marry someone with a name like that? It doesn't matter anyway. He's still dead.

I was getting cabin fever. A high temperature and a rash would have been better. That would probably be a virus. This fever was from boredom, endless, unremitting boredom. I was allergic to being alone.

I had a supply of 1080; I had the Glock. What I didn't have was the opportunity to use them. And I wanted to use them. I surely did.

The only times I left the apartment were to check the mail under my new name, Marvin Winters, and buy the paper. I liked to read a real newspaper and do the crossword puzzle. It was something I used to do every morning at GDT. I'd settle down with a coffee in the café where GDT had its offices. That was before Huntington and that damned Jacoby fired me.

The best time to check the local cafes for leftover newspapers, especially ones with a business section and crossword puzzle, was late morning before the early lunch crowd arrived. On one of these mornings, I saw a news item in the *Times* that made my head spin. It was just a sentence in an article on GDT. I kept up with the old place. I was still planning to deal with Huntington and Jacoby. But that morning, in that news article, an item read that Rachal Groes, a distant cousin of the late Brad Groes, had been appointed to the board of directors at GDT. I felt a surge of energy reading about the new board member of Global Development Technologies—and a sudden urge to have coffee with her.

I went on the internet as soon as I got back to my room. I searched the *Times* and the *P-I* online. I searched for Rachal Groes. That's how I found out about Rob Emanuel, a criminal attorney with Bauer, Bartholomew, Birnbaum, and Braun.

As I rutted through website after website, I ran across another name from my past. Spencer Granady. Well, what do ya' know? The little shit used to work for Rob Emanuel. There was Morton Jacoby, a partner at the same law firm. Jesus, all these people were after me. But they didn't know that I knew about them. Now I could add Emanuel. Yeah, I'd kill Emanuel. The "criminal attorney" was a dead man and didn't know it.

I began planning like the old days, in Minnesota, when I was in school. My first target was Rob Emanuel. I'd use the gun. Then I'd kill the girlfriend, Groes. I decided to keep the 1080 for both Huntington and Jacoby. Murder by Gift Basket. What a concept.

But, where to go next? Cuba? No, a bunch of communists. The Bahamas? Jesus, it's right in the middle of the Atlantic Ocean. Not for me. Uruguay. That's where I'd go. Uruguay. I never heard of anyone going to Uruguay. Reservations in the name of Marvin Winters. Plane tickets for a round trip of course. They were cheaper that way and would throw the cops off if they thought I might be returning. I needed a passport. I'd have to call on one of my former pilots who had a side gig getting passports. Well, I would pay him handsomely. Then we'd have a cup of coffee. Couldn't have anyone know where I obtained my passport.

Except for the passport, I was ready. I called Emanuel's office. They told me that Mr. Emanuel was due back after lunch.

The parking garage was unremarkable except for slots reserved for "Partners." I parked as close as I could to the "Partners" and waited. I was right there when Emanuel pulled in. I hadn't felt this good in months.

It was after six when Emanuel left the building. I was two cars behind when he pulled out of the garage. A dark gray, nondescript car pulled out on my tail as I left the garage. Emanuel was on his cell phone talking the entire trip to the townhouse. Christ, what a way to drive. I'm going to do a service for Seattle by getting rid of him. He's a hazard. I lost the tail by the time I reached Emanuel's apartment or condo or whatever.

He pulled into the driveway beneath the first floor. As he got out of the car, I drove directly behind him. I got off three shots, hitting the lawyer all three times. Then I jerked the car into reverse and jammed my foot on the gas. I almost hit the shabby old car that was turning into the driveway. I wanted to shoot the driver, but I knew I had to get away.

CHAPTER
FORTY-FIVE

SAM WATLAMONT

I was driving an old Pontiac, once my pride and joy, now discontinued. I avoided a collision, stopping before I rear-ended Rob's car. I jumped out and ran over to Rob, who was lying prone in a pool of blood. The pulse in Rob's neck was fast and weak. There was so much blood, I couldn't tell where the entry wounds were.

Rob was unresponsive even as I turned him over and began CPR. I had no idea how long I was compressing Rob's chest. I wasn't aware the cops had arrived until I was pulled off and away. A detective also covered in blood was yelling that the EMTs were taking over. I could stop now.

I was shaking. I couldn't take my eyes off Rob, but there was an IV going, a breathing tube was in his throat, and Rob's coat had been cut off. He was on the ambulance gurney when I last saw him. The cop hadn't left my side.

He asked if I was okay.

"Yeah, yeah. Are you going with him?"

"No, my partner will. I'm John Long. Who are you?"

"Sam Watlamont. I have a trucking business."

"Just passing by, Sam?"

"No. I've been following Mr. Emanuel. I know that sounds bad, but it was to protect him. I fucked this up, didn't I?"

"Doesn't make any sense to me, Sam. Probably above my pay grade," he said.

I looked over at him, a blood-soaked detective who looked old enough to retire. "Somehow, Detective, I think you're full of it. Can I have my one phone call before you take me downtown?"

"Sam, you're not under arrest. You can make as many calls as you want. Don't you want to clean up first?"

"Yeah, I do. But I need to make a call first." For the first time, I realized that I was as blood-soaked as the detective. I pulled out my cell and called Angie.

"Angie, honey. I'll be home soon, but you've got to call Shelley Garçon. Tell him that Mr. Emanuel's been shot. Rachal's still in Bellingham. She doesn't know."

I went to my car. John Long was right behind me.

CHAPTER
FORTY-SIX

Henry Atkinson

H enry, it's Shelley. Can you talk?"
"I just dropped my writing partner at his place. He's got to sleep off our collaboration. On the way to meet Carolyn now. What's going on?"

"I was doing inventory in the store when Angie Warren called. Rob Emanuel's been shot. On his way to Harborview. Rachal's in Bellingham at the Bellwether Hotel. She doesn't know yet. I'm going to call her now," Shelley said.

"Don't. I'll be there in about two hours," I said, and I hung up.

I had stayed in Seattle, writing and re-writing. The alcoholic former ballplayer I'd found was an unending source of stories about the Pilots. I carefully plied him with enough spirits to get good stories but keep him alive and out of the DTs. This writing was hard work.

I called Carolyn to let her know, then I filled the car with gas and headed to Bellingham. Carolyn went to Harborview.

"Earl Sedlik pledges to use all of the capabilities of his office to assist in the search for the coward who shot Rob Emanuel," I heard as I drove. The damn news was all over the radio.

I was very conservative by nature. Well, except for running off with a stranger and then marrying her. There was also the occasional violence when I hung out with Shelley. Marian and Carolyn allege that this aggression came from my long years as a patent attorney.

Whatever the source, I made the ninety miles to Bellingham in less than two hours. I hadn't called Rachal, preferring to speak to her face-to-face. She was sitting outside with a book and a glass of Pinot Grigio. When she recognized me walking out to see her, she seemed surprised, delighted, and concerned.

"Henry, what a surprise. Is Carolyn with you?"

"Rachal, there's no other way for me to tell you. Carolyn's with Rob at Harborview Hospital. He's in surgery. He's been shot." Rachal tried to get up, but I gently sat her back down.

"The doctors are the staff surgeons at the medical school. They're the best. They told Carolyn that the quick response by the police and the guy who did CPR saved his life," I said. "I've come here to bring you to him. Let's get a quick bite to eat and check out."

Rachal looked numb. She stared at me as if I was an alien from one of Saturn's rings. As if this couldn't be real.

She stood up and made a sudden move to get around me, knocking over a side table in her haste. I caught up to her within a few steps. She was crying, yelling, and flailing at me as I held her calmly, without response.

Two men stood as if to intervene. Everyone else there was struck silent. Her sobs echoed across the patio. A managerial sort of man dressed in a managerial sort of way rushed out from the lobby desk.

"Hold on there, you. Hold on there. Are you OK, Ms. Groes? Are you OK? Should I call security?"

He kept approaching and stepping back. I didn't look at him, all the while holding Rachal as her frenzy spent itself. When the fury played out, I slowly walked her to the desk, followed by the very confused hotel manager.

"Mr. Shodforen, could you please send some sandwiches and coffee to my room? I'm going to have to check out as soon as possible. Mr. Atkinson shall be assisting me," Rachal said when she calmed down a bit.

"Are you sure you're alright? Of course, you're alright. You're ordering sandwiches. Any type of sandwich, Ms. Groes? Any type of sandwich?"

"BLTs will be fine. They're for Mr. Atkinson and me. Be sure you add them to the bill." She looked at me, as we walked to the elevators. As the doors closed, I pushed the button for her floor.

"Is he always like that?"

"Oh yes. Oh yes." Rachal looked at me and smiled before she began to cry once more.

I let her cry. This was a necessary cry, not the panic-stricken sobbing that had overcome her outside. When we got to her room, she stood in the center of the room and slowly looked around. I began to pull out her luggage and talk.

"Rachal, I called Carolyn before I got out of the car. The lead surgeon had just come out to talk to her. Rob is in stable but critical condition. The bullets hit his left shoulder, the left lung, and the left buttock. He was shot in the back as he was getting out of his car."

The food arrived, packaged for travel. The manager said he would forward the bill. Twice.

"The guy who did the CPR also thinks he can identify the shooter. So, things are bad, but not terrible. We just need to get on the road. We can eat in the car. Do I need to repeat myself?"

For that, I did get hit, but she laughed. As we were about to leave, the room phone rang. Rachal picked it up on speaker phone.

"Hello? This is Rachal Groes."

"Good afternoon, Ms. Groes. My name is John Long. I'm a detective with the Seattle Police Department. I was told where you were by Sam Watlamont."

"I know Mr. Watlamont. Before you go on, detective, is this about my fiancée?"

"Yes, it is. Has someone informed you of his condition?" the cop asked.

"Yes. And I'm in the process of leaving right now to return to Seattle. I assume you'll want to speak with me, but can I ask to meet you at the hospital? I'm anxious to get on my way."

"Of course. I can meet you there. Are you driving?"

"As soon as I can," Rachal said.

"You just be careful, Ms. Groes. Check out the *P-I*'s list of speed traps on I-5 before you go. I'm looking forward to meeting you." He hung up, leaving Rachal staring at the phone.

"That was a cop wishing me a good trip and telling me to check out a list of speed traps. Do you think that was for real?" Rachal asked me

"You check it out while I drive. I hate those damn things."

CHAPTER
FORTY-SEVEN

CAROLYN ATKINSON

I felt the pressure. Was I getting old? Would I get a byline on this story? Or was I part of the story? Was I now a mother hen, sent to look after the young ones? Here I was, racing to the hospital to check on Rob.

I was increasingly concerned that Rachal might have heard the hysteria being spread on the airwaves. I identified myself as a friend of Rob's from the office. The hospital volunteer directed me to the corner where a young woman was sitting by herself using her cell phone. A few minutes later, the call was disconnected, and we introduced ourselves.

The woman was Angie Warren, Sam Watlamont's girlfriend. Sam had done CPR on Rob Emanuel. He was with the detective, answering questions about his relationship with Rob. I let her talk even though I knew much of what she was saying.

As she continued, Angie broke down several times. "Sam was trying to help protect Mr. Emanuel. He always felt he couldn't repay Mr. Emanuel for getting him acquitted when he was arrested. Sam's devastated.

"He made a deal with someone named Shelley to continue to follow Mr. Emanuel. We've been getting a check every month from Shelley. Now, this," she said. "Do you think the police will think Sam had something to do with shooting Mr. Emanuel?" She began to cry again.

"Angie, listen to me. Shelley's my husband's cousin. I'm here to see after you and find out about Mr. Emanuel. My husband, Henry, is on the way to check on Rob's fiancée. Sam not only didn't do anything wrong, but I'll bet the doctors think he saved Rob's life. The cops will think so too."

We looked at each other without saying anything. Angie kept trying to stop crying. I got two phone calls while we were together. Henry had arrived in Bellingham and was trying to calm Rachal. They would be at the hospital in about three hours. The next call was from Shelley. He and Marian were on the way to Boston for the first flight they could get to Seattle. He'd call again from SeaTac.

Shelley was upset. He wanted to get Nolan Herbert. This wasn't a random shooting. It wasn't some moron shooting in the air. Sam had seen Herbert firing directly into Emanuel. It was cold-blooded attempted murder. Shelley was angry. Not a good thing.

The detective with Sam Watlamont came to Harborview to see how Rob was doing. They came to see Angie and me first. Angie took one look at Sam and started to cry again. He took her aside for a few minutes and then she drove him home. I was now there by myself, though I wasn't exactly alone.

Randall came by with Stan Wight from GDT. Mort Jacoby was still in the law office when he got the news and then Ubered over. Most of the BB and BB staff began arriving in the waiting room soon after. Maryann Wilson dropped by to pay her respects and then drove Randall home. Mort didn't look well, so Stan took him, and I called Gail to alert her.

The detective wasn't sure who I was, but he had taken Mort aside for a few minutes before he left. He got my bona fides and agreed to have Rob's secretary send him a list of Rob's clients. He came back to sit with me. Frankly, it was annoying. I just wanted to be there for Rachal when she arrived.

The surgeon and I had been talking. He was about to go when Long returned.

"Detective, good to see you again. Still refusing to take that promotion?" the surgeon asked him. They seemed to know each other.

"Yeah. I can't stand the uniform. I like the hours better, too. Make my own," the detective said.

"Well, we missed you the last few weeks. Comin' over Tuesday?"

"I'll sure try. You still have those big lamb chops on Tuesdays?"

"He's convinced pork chops are large lamb chops," the surgeon said. Long had a look of faux surprise. "I'll make certain we will. See you then."

He turned to me. "Ms. Atkinson, you tell this guy what I told you, will you? I've got to see our patient in recovery before he goes to ICU." He turned and left before anyone responded, limping into the recovery room.

"He's younger than I am. Can't fix his knees though. Damn shame," the detective said and sighed. "You know, there are some citizens I have to arrest, some of whom have been injured, shall we say. Often, they're brought here to Harborview." He pointed to the ICU doors. "That man fixes 'em up. He does such a good job they can leave the hospital and engage Mr. Emanuel as a defense attorney. Seattle's a small town in many ways."

I'd been waiting to bring him up-to-date on Rob's surgery. The cop started to reminisce about growing up when the city was like a large town. When I heard him bring up the Seattle Pilots, I had to smile.

I stood up and excused myself. I went down to the cafeteria for the dreadful hospital coffee, a well-known redundancy. Henry was due in the next half hour, but I had no idea when Marian and Shelley would arrive.

When I returned to the waiting room, I found the detective sitting near the elevator, reading yesterday's paper. I was a little surprised.

"Detective, if I had known you'd still be here, I would have brought some coffee."

"No, thank you, Ms. Atkinson. I didn't know I had offended you that much. I do apologize." He stood and walked with me back to the table and chairs where I had spent the early part of the evening with Angie.

"You mean because I might have brought coffee?" I asked.

"Ma'am, around these parts, that's considered a threat."

Despite the surroundings, I laughed.

"You waiting for anyone, in particular, Ms. Atkinson?"

"It's Mrs. But please call me Carolyn. I'm waiting for my husband. He's bringing Rachal, Mr. Emanuel's fiancée. She and Rob had been staying in Bellingham for a few days when Rob was called back for some sort of a hearing. He was going to return in the morning. When Henry, my husband, and I heard what happened, he went to get her, and I came here," I explained.

"Pardon my curiosity, Ms.—sorry, Mrs.—Atkinson, but how did you two become so involved with them? Are you family?"

"No. We came here to research a book my husband is writing about the Seattle Pilots. We have a few acquaintances here as well and met Rob and Rachal through them."

"I assume that Mort Jacoby is one of those acquaintances?" the detective said.

"We met him through Stanford Wight, a law school classmate of my husband when they were recruiting Randall Huntington. And before you ask, I met that young lady who was here when I walked in."

"It's somewhat convoluted, but I think I've got it. Thank you. I have a feeling we may run into one another again. If you or your husband think I can be of any help, I can be reached through Earl Sedlik's office."

He handed me his card and walked back to the elevator. A harried young woman was coming out as he was about to hit the button. He pointed her over to me and entered the empty car.

Rachal started to walk in my direction before she stopped for a moment and looked back where Long had been standing. She shook her head and bumped into me as I walked to greet her.

"Carolyn, where is he? Where's Rob? Is he out of surgery yet? Is he OK?"

"He's in recovery before they take him to the ICU. The surgery went well. They'll tell us when he's moved to ICU."

Rachal dissolved into a tearful mess, holding onto me. I slowly moved her to the chairs around a table near the recovery room entrance. That's where we were when Henry came in from parking the car.

CHAPTER
FORTY-EIGHT

Nolan Herbert

Marvin Winters, as I preferred to be called, didn't think about speed traps. I backed out of the driveway like I was a test driver in a television ad. Then I hit the brakes and pulled the wheel to the left. I jammed my foot on the gas, barely missing the dark gray, nondescript sedan driving toward me. I wanted to shoot the driver, but I knew it would take too much time. Instead, I forced the old jalopy to the side of the road as I flew out of the neighborhood.

I ran several red lights before I slowed down and turned into traffic. I settled into the starts and stops of the complexities of daily life. No one noticed anything about me or my car. I was just another impediment to getting home, a turd in a sea of them.

I was feeling good, euphoric. Three shots into Emanuel's back and a clean getaway, except for that damn old car I forced over. Even that didn't worry me. I had obscured the license plates. I'd be dumping the car soon anyway.

The girlfriend was next. Rachal Groes probably thought she was a princess. Inherited Brad's money and probably voted with Huntington. Didn't matter anymore. I'd kill her just like I killed her boyfriend. Shit, she never worked a day in her life for that money. It was all because of me, Nolan Herbert. I deserved the money.

The traffic was better. I turned onto a residential street across town from where poor Rob Emanuel met his end. I parked in a darkened driveway, left the keys on the passenger seat, and got out with my briefcase. I walked down the street. I had to control myself from whistling.

I walked back to the main drag and waited for a bus. I changed buses twice until I saw an open used car lot. The cars were awful, but the sign above said, "Kwik loan approval." That made them look better.

I had a wad of cash on me. I walked around the well-lit lot until I saw a fairly new model, one that looked like it could be driven for some time. As I walked toward the office, an over-enthusiastic salesman approached me.

"Like that one, mister? It's a beauty. Want to get in and get a better look?"

"No, I like it fine. I'll take it."

The expression on the salesman's face was a true surprise. "You sure you don't want to get in?"

"No. I want it. Can we go inside and do the paperwork?"

"Sure, sure. And who do I have the pleasure of talking to?"

"Marvin Winters. Got any coffee in there?"

CHAPTER
FORTY-NINE

RACHAL GROES

The US attorney for the Western District of Washington walked out of the elevator, paused as he got his bearings, and walked over to me. I wasn't sure how he knew me. I guess he had seen pictures, but, still, he knew me at once. I was on edge, jumping up at any sound that might be from beyond the ICU doors. I was anxious, nervous, and scared. My hair was coming undone, my face was swollen, my eyes were red.

The attorney hesitated briefly as he left the elevator and then made a beeline toward me. Henry stiffened as he saw this stranger approach us.

Sedlik seemed to take note of the Atkinsons, who must have appeared protective as he got closer to us. He slowed and changed his gait, subtly becoming an important official rather than a family friend.

Henry watched the transformation. As Sedlik approached, Henry stood to meet him and take his measure. The two men locked eyes briefly. Henry put his hand out.

"Hi, I'm Henry Atkinson. Are you looking for somebody? We've been here a while, and I can point out some of our fellow inmates. The hospital volunteer has already left for the day."

"Thank you, Mr. Atkinson, but this is the young lady I've come to see. Ms. Groes, I'm Earl Sedlik, a friend of Rob's. How is he?" he asked.

Over the next hour, we talked. I knew who he was. I knew how Rob had been trying to get him involved in going after Nolan Herbert.

"Have you caught him yet? Nolan Herbert? That's who shot Rob. Have you arrested him?" I sounded frantic. I was.

"We have a manhunt underway. I'm also arranging a bodyguard for you, Ms. Groes. We found an abandoned car earlier tonight. Inside, there was a notebook with your name in it. You, Mort Jacoby, and Randall Huntington are his next targets. The police are covering those two also."

I was shocked. I had never considered that I might be in the line of fire. The utter madness of Herbert became clear. And there wasn't anything I could do. Anyway, I wasn't going to be leaving the hospital.

Henry and Carolyn had been peripheral to the conversation. Carolyn made a point of checking the time.

"Rachal, honey. You and Henry had a long drive. Why don't we get you home?"

"No, thank you. I'm not leaving. Henry, would you mind bringing my bags in? I'll be able to clean up and stay in the waiting room. I'm staying here."

A uniformed officer came over to us. He said a few words to Sedlik, who excused himself and left. The cop introduced himself and walked over to a chair nearby. I assumed he was my watchdog.

Henry went to the car for my things. Carolyn tried once more to get me to come with them, unsuccessfully. They left as I took out my toiletry bag. I asked my keeper to watch the rest of my belongings, and I retreated to the ladies' room.

CHAPTER
FIFTY

NOLAN HERBERT

I was hanging around the café at the Frye Museum, practicing writing my new name. I made a few phone calls, one of which was to one of my pilots from Air Germination. The guy who would get a passport for Marvin so I could go on to Uruguay. I was worried about what to do with the pilot, but that was for later.

Earlier in the afternoon, as I was cruising around Harborview, I'd seen a woman run into the emergency room entrance. She looked like Rachal Groes. It was difficult to know from a picture in the newspaper, but I knew. That's when I went to the museum. It wasn't far from the hospital, and I was able to read and practice my penmanship while killing time.

I waited until visiting hours were over, figuring that Rachal would have to be dragged out before she'd leave. There shouldn't be anyone else who might know me there. I tucked the gun into my jacket and left the museum bistro.

I walked over to the main entrance. There wasn't any reason to make a scene by using the ER. I wanted things to be peaceful. I was a peaceable kind of guy.

Rachal was sitting near the doors to the ICU. She was sitting with a couple I'd never seen before. This pissed me off. It wasn't part of my plan. I liked my schemes to go as I intended. I hadn't even brought any 1080 with me. This would never do.

I was sitting close to the elevator with a clear view of Rachal, Sedlik, and the busybodies. I saw a uniform cop approach them and sit down. I waited until Rachal was alone except for the "watcher," but it was clear that he wasn't leaving. Damn. I couldn't shoot them both.

I walked back to the museum parking lot. It was almost empty. There was one other car. It was one of those cars that looked abandoned, like someone parked, locked up, and went to see the Degas exhibit but never returned. I would have stolen it, but who knew how long it had been there. Maybe there was a bomb underneath. Could have been. There are some crazy people out there.

I went to my tiny apartment. I had to start packing. Except for my passport, things were coming together. I had had to add two others to my list, but I still had enough 1080.

According to the instructions that came with the Glock, it was supposed to be cleaned after firing. Then I would reload it. I wanted to keep it loaded.

CHAPTER
FIFTY-ONE

MORT JACOBY

I was having whiskey, straight up. It was an expensive bottle, and I'd earned it, goddammit. I was the oldest partner in BB and BB. I was on the board at GDT.

It wasn't my first drink of the evening. I was in my home office, brooding. What's the expression? "Six degrees of separation?" Well, one of my partners had been shot. An old friend of mine operated on him. Another friend was in charge of the investigation. I'm a well-known attorney at law, and all I could do was drink whiskey, straight up. I didn't know how many degrees that was, but I wasn't feeling too well, from the whiskey or my powerlessness. Hell, I was afraid to stand up.

It was almost midnight when my cell phone rang. I thought my wife was in bed. Our kids lived in nearby towns with their own families. This was an area code I didn't know. It could be someone calling to assist my complaint against the IRS, which I hadn't filed, or an agent to help with my Medicare Advantage plan, which I didn't have. With luck, it might be a wrong number. I'd had just enough whiskey to want to speak to a wrong number.

"Hello, I think you have a wrong number. I do hope the rest of your evening improves." I wasn't feeling any pain about this time.

"Mort, it's me, Henry Atkinson, don't hang up." I hung up.

Henry tried again. This time I stayed on the line. Well, I couldn't find the landline base to hang up. Henry was trying to warn me about something.

"Mort, are you still with me?"

"Henry, you kidder. Are you here? How did you get in? Do you want a drink?"

"Let's keep talking, Mort. Try to guess where I am." I heard him tell somebody that my speech was "thlurred." That pithed me off.

"You thound really clothe. Is Carolyn with you?" I asked.

"She's right here, buddy. She's right here."

Henry kept talking. I couldn't hang up. That's rude. I decided to sit on the floor.

CHAPTER
FIFTY-TWO

CAROLYN ATKINSON

I'd followed the GPS to the Jacoby house. Henry and I had to trust the cop at the hospital to watch over Rachal. She trusted him.

I texted Marian while Henry drove. Her phone rang almost at once.

"Marian, where are you?"

"Getting a car at SeaTac. Where are you?"

"On the way to see Mort Jacoby. There's a city cop with Rachal at the hospital. The US attorney got the county attorney to send out police to watch her, Jacoby, and Randall Huntington. Mort didn't sound well. He's been drinking himself under the table. His wife's beside herself," I said.

"Any word on Herbert?"

"No, except an abandoned car was found earlier tonight that must have belonged to him. There was a notebook inside with plans to kill Rachal after killing Rob, then go after Jacoby and Randall. That's why police are watching them.

"Henry called Gail when Mort stopped talking. She didn't know about Rob until Mort came home and started to drink."

"Carolyn, we're headed into the city now. Shelley got a room at your hotel. See you for breakfast," Marian said.

There was an unmarked car in front of the Jacobys' house when Henry pulled up. The cop was out with his weapon in hand as we got out of the car.

"Excuse me. Please stop where you are and place both hands against the car. Now." The officer was polite but firm.

We stopped in our tracks. We turned toward the police flashlight and froze. The light stayed on us. We realized this was the police protection assigned to Mort. We put our hands on the car.

"Ma'am, let your purse down, slowly. Now, Mister, raise your hands and walk over to where the lady is." He watched Henry as he walked to my side of the car. We were now leaning on the passenger side of the car.

"Do either of you have a weapon?" He was standing behind us and reached for my pocketbook.

"What are your names and why are you here? It's a little late for a social call."

"My name is Henry Atkinson, and this is my wife, Carolyn. Can I take my wallet out to show my identification?"

"Take your wallet out with two fingers," the cop said.

He had to reach under his sport coat to his left rear pants pocket. He pulled the wallet out with his thumb and forefinger and held it over his head. The cop took it and quickly opened it to his identification. He asked me to do the same with my purse, which he placed on the hood of the car.

"Mr. and Mrs. Atkinson, can you tell me why you're here at this time of night?"

"One of the reasons was to see if you or someone like you was here yet. Earl Sedlik told us that he was sending officers out. The other was to check on Morton Jacoby. His wife is concerned about his drinking, and we're all friends."

The cop gave us our wallets back and walked us to the front door. He rang the bell and waited with us. Within seconds, lights went on inside the house, and then outside.

"Henry, Carolyn. Who is that with you?"

"Mrs. Jacoby, I'm Officer Roberts with SPD. Are these two people friends of yours?"

"Yes. I've been expecting them. Can they come in now?" Gail asked.

Officer Roberts stood back, holstered his weapon, and said good night. Henry thanked the cop for being thorough. When the door was closed, a pajama-clad Gail pulled me into a hug and then Henry.

Gail led us into the den. There was Mort, snoring on the floor with a makeshift pillow under his head, the phone still in his hand. Two empty bottles of scotch whiskey completed the tableau. Gail began to cry.

"He's never been drunk. He drinks too much, but he's never been drunk. Look at him. He began drinking when he got home from the hospital. I can't lift him."

"First of all, help us get him to bed. Then Carolyn and I can clean up in here. I don't know what happened. I do know that he's going to be sick in the morning," Henry said. "We'll stay if you need us, but that cop or another one will be here twenty-four hours a day until Herbert is caught. There is also security with Rachal and Randall as of tonight.

"The cops found Herbert's car with his notebook inside. They'll get him. Until then, you'll have a full-time sitter. When Mort's well enough, reassure him of that."

It took over an hour to get Mort to bed. Gail got him undressed and into his PJs. Henry and I were able to clean up. We also hid several more bottles of booze. We said our goodnights to Gail and left. The cop was awake, watching us as we pulled away.

CHAPTER
FIFTY-THREE

Henry Atkinson

Carolyn and I found Shelley in the dining room. He had been the first one up and settled in for breakfast. He had *The Seattle Times* to keep him company, and it did. He saw a story in the second section about a used car salesman who was found dead at his desk at work. The medical examiner ruled it was likely a heart attack. It seems that the salesman had completed a sale and was doing the paperwork. No one else was in the office at the time. A half a cup of lukewarm coffee was sitting on the desk.

Carolyn and I were sitting down when Shelley looked up at us.

"Didn't you bring your legal pad?"

I thought that was a funny way to say good morning, but Shelley didn't do funny. The newspaper was opened on the table. Shelley pointed to the article on the death of the salesman in a used car lot.

"Doesn't smell right, Henry. Forty-seven-year-old guy. An unfinished cup of coffee on his desk. The preliminary cause of death . . ."

"A heart attack." I finished the sentence, then picked up the paper.

"I wonder if a car is missing." Carolyn tied it up again.

Marian had joined us and looked up from the menu. "Who's heading up the search for Herbert?"

I called for the waiter. I'd become very impatient. "I haven't the slightest idea, but I know who will."

We ordered quickly. When the waiter left and the coffee and pastry tray was finished, I pulled out my phone.

"Good morning. Can you transfer me to the ICU waiting room, please?"

"Is Emanuel able to speak?" Marian was dubious.

"No, but Rachal's been there all night. She'll know," I said.

Rachal picked up the phone. "Rachal, good morning. How's Rob?"

"Better. The breathing tube was removed, and he's breathing on his own. He woke up and knew me. They had to lighten up on his morphine, but he is on a pump that he can push every so often. He's asleep now," she said.

"Shelley just told me that the pump's called a PCA pump. Patient-controlled anesthesia. It sounds like things are moving along well. Can we pick you up and get you home to clean up and change clothes?"

"No, I'm not ready, Henry."

"Carolyn can stay there. Rob's getting better. It's time for you to get some sleep in a real bed."

"Henry, you're probably right. Let's see how he is when you get here. I can't think about leaving right now," she said.

"OK, but I do have a question first. Do you know who's in charge of the investigation? We have some things we want to discuss."

"Well, overall, it's John Long from the prosecuting attorney's office to run things on the ground. He's an old friend of Mort Jacoby if you need more information."

"Rachal, we'll be there a little after noon. Is that cop still watching you?" I asked.

"Yes, he is. Should be a change of shift soon. Remember when you tried to explain your theory of investigations being like baseball? Long quiet spells, then a flurry of activity. Are any men on base now?"

"Rachal, you have some memory. Yeah, there are two men on base, the crowd is standing, the best hitter is up, and a new pitcher is coming in. The game is on."

I got Long's number from Rachal. Then Carolyn called Gail Jacoby to check on Mort, who had slept through the night. He was awake but dealing with a major league hangover. He couldn't talk, a noteworthy manifestation of a serious disorder in a lawyer, even a corporate lawyer. Carolyn gave me one of her looks. I slowed the car, pulled over, and checked the GPS. We went to see if Gail needed an extra hand.

The unmarked car was still out front. The cop was watching us from the second we drove up until Gail let us in. Mort was sitting on the side of the bed. Somehow, he looked worse than disheveled. He had a lethal expression for anyone who caught his eye. All in all, he appeared to be indignant, in pain, and in his own awful world. I offered to help him up. Carolyn and Gail didn't. They left the room.

I tried to get Mort to stand, which almost brought both of us down. Mort was awake, based on the unintelligible sounds coming from him. But he was a living, breathing dead weight. We were sitting on the bed before Mort could talk.

I tried to ask a question. Mort turned and looked at me.

"Why didn't you just ask me to get up instead of trying to kill us both?" he said.

I was surprised but controlled myself. "How well do you know John Long?"

"We grew up together. He was contrary when we were twelve years old. Never changed. Refuses to be promoted because he doesn't want to wear a uniform, even for funerals. That kind of ornery. Great cop. Works as the chief investigator on cases like this one with Rob Emanuel." He was getting short of breath.

"He ever go out drinking with you like you did last night?"

"No, goddammit. Now why don't you get the hell out of here. If I'm lucky, I'll throw up all over you." He started to slide back down the bed.

"That would be terrific, counselor. I'm confident your wife would be overjoyed. Come with me, and let's go to the bathroom." I pulled him back up. It was a struggle, but we made it. I held my host by the back of his shirt and splashed him with water. Mort's speech became very clear. It was enough to embarrass a drunken sailor, flawless in diction and meaning. I was never that erudite.

Eventually, Mort was able to help himself. His clothes and most of the *en suite*, including me, were soaked, but he could change into jeans and a pull over. I could only hope to dry sooner rather than later.

Over coffee, Mort filled us in on what had gone on, most of which we had learned from Rachal. I felt better about Long. I went to the den and called the man himself to discuss the car salesman.

"Detective, you don't know me or my cousin. I get that. But think of the fact that Rob Emanuel had been talking to the US attorney about a series of suspicious 'heart attacks' right after having coffee with Nolan Herbert. Have you checked to see if there is a car missing from the lot? I bet there is. I think it was taken by Herbert after he poisoned the salesman. Check the coffee."

I returned from the den and spoke to Mort. "That was Long. We discussed Nolan Herbert. I see Carolyn has shown you the item about the used car salesman. We think Herbert killed him by poisoning his coffee.

"Gail, I think Mort should stay home for a few days. Herbert is out there somewhere. Abrams confirmed that there are cops watching Mort, Randall, and Rachal around the clock.

"We're going to see what we can find out without getting in the way of the police. Shelley's out there with an old client of Rob's right now. We'll be in touch."

CHAPTER
FIFTY-FOUR

SHELLEY GARÇON

S am Watlamont made his living driving his rig on contract runs along the coast from Seattle to San Francisco and back. Before that, he drove a pick-up doing small jobs in the city. He knew his way around without GPS or maps, those paper relics which could never be refolded. Driving around Seattle with Sam was an education.

We were on our own manhunt, which included a visit to the used car lot, which was being considered a crime scene because of the stolen car. It was wrapped in sagging yellow police tape when we got there. There were only a few empty spaces where cars had been.

An agitated man in a bad suit kept walking around the perimeter, talking on his cell phone. He noticed us leaning on a dusty sedan and watching him.

"What do you two want? Can't you see I'm closed? Are you with the press? Get out of here."

He was screeching at us. We didn't respond. He walked toward us, yelling all the way.

"Mister, you're going to wake the dead, if you'll pardon me saying?" Sam spoke in an even tone. At his height, he didn't need to yell.

"I'm going to call the cops. You two are harassing me. What are you doing here?"

"Calm down. You'll have a stroke. Take some deep breaths. You'll be OK." I startled Bad Suit when I spoke, but I still hadn't moved.

"All right. See, I'm quiet and taking deep breaths. Now get out of here. You're creeping me out," the man said.

"We're getting along much better now, aren't we? We just have a couple of questions for you. Then we'll be on our way. Right?" I turned to Sam, who nodded silently.

"I gotta go to the bathroom. Make it quick," the man told us.

"That's more than we wanted to know. But here goes. What kind of car was missing from the lot when you got here? And was there any paperwork filled out with the name of the last customer?" I asked.

"You're cops. Shit. I shoulda known. Your buddies have all that stuff. They were here for hours."

"They do. They're good cops. It's the lieutenant— doesn't trust anything we do. Sends out backups to check on the uniforms. That's us. So, tell us what we need to know, and we'll let you go to the head," I said.

"Jesus H. Christ. The cops don't trust the cops. What's a citizen like me to do?"

"Give us what we need, or you'll shit in your pants, sir."

"OK, yeah. The car was, is, oh, you know what I mean, a red Dodge Challenger, 2017 model. My guy was layin' on some papers. Best I could tell before the cops threw me out of my own damn business, the customer was Winters. Marvin or Mervin Winters. Maybe it was Walters. I don't know. Your buddies threw me out of my own shop. Happy now? Get out of here." He was yelling again. He ran across the street to a diner. Probably had a bathroom.

Sam and I waited for our new friend to get back from the bathroom. He took one look at us and started to go in the other direction. He couldn't outrun Sam, who brought him back.

"Our apologies, sir, but the looey won't let us leave you alone until you get us the license plate number and the VIN. Then we're out of here. Aren't we, partner?" My sincerity was somewhere between glib and cringing. I could be really good like that sometimes.

We got what we needed and called it to Henry. We went to the diner across the street and started to look for Marvin or Mervin Winters or Walters. Sam's knowledge of the city eliminated several possibilities by the addresses. We finally decided on one Marvin Winters, one Marvin Walters, and a Mervin Winters.

I called the identification of the car to John Long. He told me that the ticket taker at the hospital garage thought he saw a sporty red Dodge leave the garage. Police activity in Greater Seattle increased. An all-points lookout for a red, 2017 Dodge Challenger being driven by a middle-aged male was posted.

CHAPTER
FIFTY-FIVE

Nolan Herbert

I was a new man. I was Marvin Winters. I bought a pair of purple scrubs as a going away gift to Nolan Herbert that morning. I really liked how I looked. The scrubs looked crisp, and my shoes were polished. My watch was an Omega. I even stopped for a manicure before I went to the hospital. There I was, hiding in the open. There wasn't a sign of the old Nolan. Marvin was lookin' good.

The vials of 1080 were in my messenger bag. It was leather and all the rage. I parked in the visitor section of one of the garages serving the hospital. No one stopped me as I entered the hospital. I rode the elevator and picked floors at random to walk down.

It took three floors before I found a tray delivery cart. I started to push it to a service elevator when I heard someone yelling behind me. Silly man.

I arrived at an open elevator which I promptly entered and rode to the ICU floor. I was about to follow a tech or male nurse when I noticed the Groes woman. Her legs were tucked up beneath her, a blanket spread over her lap. A book appeared to be sliding from her hand.

I parked the cart and walked to the coffee table along the side wall. It hadn't been straightened up in a while. I brushed off the table and tossed some stirrers into the trash. I poured the contents of one of my vials into a cup and then filled it with coffee. I wasn't sure if she liked cream with her coffee, so I brought powdered creamer with me. I brought the coffee and creamer to her. She was watching me as she picked up the book, which had fallen from her lap.

She must have seen me preparing the already lethal cup of yesterday's swill. As I strolled over to her, she looked at my polished black loafers with tassels and my scrubs that still had a fresh crease. These may have been a bit too much.

"Hi, I noticed that you've been here all night. Maybe this coffee will help." I tried to be ingratiating but may have come off as smarmy. She drew her legs up and wrapped her arms around them as soon as she saw me, closing herself off. Maybe she had already ID'd me as phony as a three-dollar bill. The manicured nails might have given me away. It could have been the tassels.

"Thanks. That's very nice of you. I don't think I'm ready for coffee yet. Why don't you put it down over there? I'm going to try to get some more sleep, on purpose this time." She smiled up at me.

Her smile broadened considerably when she saw her security return from the men's room. Another guard came out of the elevator and walked over to us. He stopped by the tray delivery cart that I left when I saw Rachal. He waved to the cop he was replacing. He used his cell phone to make a call before going to introduce himself to Rachal.

"Did either of you see who brought in that delivery cart? One of the dietary techs was yelling about someone stealing his cart."

I began backing away from Rachal when I saw the first uniform cop approach us. I turned and walked briskly to the first elevator with open doors.

As I got on, I heard the copper ask, "Ms. Groes, do you know that man?"

CHAPTER
FIFTY-SIX

John Long

D on't even touch that cup. I think that was Nolan Herbert." The cop who had just showed up pulled his cell phone back out and called in more officers. Within minutes, there were additional cops, including me. Rachal was tremulous when she realized how close she had been to Herbert. I sat with her as I talked to the cop who made the call. I set a table in front of us to serve as my headquarters while I was here. The business of the waiting room went on, but it went on around us.

Fingerprint specialists had arrived, and they went to work on the cart and the cup of coffee. I had the coffee sequestered separately from the cup for analysis. Another officer found the empty vial in the trash where the coffee urns were, and it went straight to the fingerprints team.

"He certainly doesn't work here, despite the scrubs. His hands are manicured, and he's wearing a very expensive watch and highly polished loafers with tassels. He said he knew I was here all night and brought me that coffee," Rachal said. She was calming down amidst the blue swarm. I hoped my presence reassured her how well she was being watched.

The hospital couldn't be shut down, but we flooded the place. Rachal and her guardian gave virtually the same description of the perp. It was sent to a police artist, and a copy came back within the hour.

I went over the conversation I had with Henry Atkinson, whoever the hell that was. It had been a real pisser. Now this cup of coffee was brought to Rachal Groes. I knew it was poison. Atkinson was right.

Where is Herbert? Another body yesterday. They're piling up. Oh, shit. Atkinson had said something about his cousin too. There's an insane killer out there, and, meanwhile, these two random cousins want to help catch him. God save me from cousins. I'll bet they're married and are bringing their wives along.

I should have taken the lieutenant's exam. They had better offices.

CHAPTER
FIFTY-SEVEN

NOLAN HERBERT

I barely made it through the visitors' garage, almost hitting the parking gate arm. I've never driven that fast, but I didn't care. I needed to get out. Horns were blaring as I left the hospital grounds. I headed northeast and suddenly made a left, heading northwest. If I could just make it to the Pike Place Market garage, I could get lost in the crowd. The traffic was building as morning rush hour was replaced by tourists in cars, vans, and buses. The ambulatory traffic became even worse as I neared Pike Place.

I suddenly realized that my bright red sports car might be calling attention to me. That was it. I couldn't hide in a car painted scarlet. I left it at a traffic light about four blocks from the Biscuit Bitch and trotted off. I think some people noticed. Damn.

It was getting hard to hide. Even wearing polished black loafers with tassels, and carrying a trendy leather messenger bag, the dark purple scrubs stood out. They did. So, I ducked into the first open tourist shop and bought a T-shirt with a flying fish. Sometimes you had to act. I stuffed the purple scrub shirt into the messenger bag.

Security was visible throughout the market. They were there to locate lost kids and direct bewildered pedestrians who wouldn't admit they were dazed and disoriented. There were other cops looking for me, but not these guys. They had their hands full.

I had to get out of there. It was getting packed. All these people were making it hard to breathe. They were breathing my air. This was my space. There were two teenage girls behind me talking about purple scrubs. I could hear them. I knew it. I turned and swung my trendy messenger bag at them. I missed, but I nailed an old lady in the back. It wasn't a total loss. She fell forward into produce. People started screaming.

I had no idea who was yelling. I shouted back and began to run, pushing at the large crowd surrounding me. I had even less air. Someone was taking my air. I was breathing faster and faster. I had to get my air. I pulled the Glock from my bag, and there was utter chaos. The crowd melted away in front of me but grew at the same time. I turned from side to side as I tried to find my way out of the market. I almost tripped. I grabbed a table full of fruit. Plums and berries flew onto the floor.

I heard sirens piercing through the cacophony of a riot. I wasn't aware of firing the pistol, but the throng dissipated almost immediately. I held the gun over my head and ran toward the street. The sound of sirens was overwhelming. I shoved the revolver into my pocket and ran through the crowd, trying to leave. Police cars had swarmed the area. Cops were fighting to gain control of the mass of people.

I saw one cop standing next to an open car door. He couldn't see me behind him. The Glock fired once. The uniformed officer fell forward. I pushed his body aside and jumped into his car. I lost time looking for the brake release, but I leaned on the accelerator. Bodies flew as I drove through the crowd. Someone was yelling in the car. I made sure the windows were closed. I turned up the air conditioner fan, but I still heard that awful yelling. I sped up the wrong way on Pine Street. It was pandemonium in the market. What a lovely word that is.

CHAPTER
FIFTY-EIGHT

Henry Atkinson

Carolyn and I were in John Long's office when he got the news of the riot at Pike Place. The detective identified him from the descriptions of the shooter. Sometimes he was in a purple scrub shirt, sometimes in a tourist fish shirt. He was driving a red car or a police car. Even with the variation, we knew it was Herbert.

The crowd noise was increasing. The base runners were taunting the pitcher who was in his windup. Casey was up to bat.

The police officer who had been shot at the market was on his way to Harborview. The chaos at the office was devolving back into a crowd. Long was cursing, apologizing to Carolyn, and cursing again in a stream of consciousness. He was agitated, pacing the room. His TV was on, his computer was airing a news station, and he was yelling at his cell phone. The shooter had stolen a police car and disappeared. Seattle's finest were stretched to the breaking point.

Ed Abrams, who was the assistant prosecuting attorney, and the police chief were on their way to Long's office. Carolyn and I tried not to draw attention to ourselves, but we quietly moved to the door. Each time we thought we had made it, someone else came in. The room was beginning to fill up like a scene from a Marx Brothers' movie.

As befits a successful politician, Earl Sedlik was the last one there. When he walked in, I held the door for him. Carolyn slipped out as I gave my regards to all and followed.

For a few seconds, the sounds in the room came to a halt. Everyone in the room stopped talking. Long stopped swearing. The room was very quiet for just that moment. Then they started yelling again . . . at each other. Carolyn and I left by the stairwell at the end of the hall. The cacophony created by these very important people continued until we closed the stairwell door.

CHAPTER
FIFTY-NINE

SHELLEY GARÇON

S am was a much better driver than I was. Much better, and he knew where he was all the time. That's how we were able to winnow down the addresses of "Marvin Winters" so quickly. I was much better at rifling the place. I found the pages where Marvin Winters was practicing his penmanship. Winters or Herbert had simply tossed page after page into the trash. There was a page with names of South American countries, and Uruguay was circled several times.

Then I found the mother lode. I found a box with cans of 1080. I had no idea what it was, but it had the international symbol of poison on the label. This could be the source of all those heart attacks. I stuffed the notebook paper into the box with the cans and a partially completed book of crossword puzzles. The more I found out about Herbert, the crazier the guy seemed.

I heard the sirens before I heard knocking on the door. It was Sam. We got out of there with what we wanted. I knew a thing or two about searching a room because I had searched a room or two. Searching is not simply looking for something. To be successful, the room couldn't look like it had been searched. Cops usually left a mess. I didn't.

Herbert wouldn't notice that his place had been rummaged through until he went to look for the 1080. The cops would know sooner, but I wore gloves and wiped up as I went. Marian never believed how neat I could be. I tried at home, but it never seemed to meet her standards.

CHAPTER
SIXTY

Marian Garçon

I was a basket case. I had gone with Shelley to pick up Sam and stayed with Angie until she had to go to work. She took me back to the hotel to wait, something I don't do well. I couldn't call my husband, who was skulking around the city with a truck driver looking for a homicidal maniac. I couldn't call my best friend Carolyn, who was supposed to be meeting with the detective leading the hunt for the homicidal maniac.

Carolyn's loving husband Henry had intended to write a book about a baseball team that went missing. I decided to write one about how Henry constantly seemed get involved with homicidal maniacs. Then all of them could become better acquainted. Henry was a patent attorney for Pete's sake. How did this always happen?

I ordered room service and pulled out one of those little note pads that hotels provide near the phone. Carolyn called to let me know they had had to cut the meeting short and would meet me for lunch. Shit, there goes room service.

I made my way down to the casual dining room that looked out on the street. It was a very pleasant place, especially after the lunch crowd had dispersed. I was going to make some notes about my possible book. I got distracted by the bizarre sight of a police car riding with two wheels on the sidewalk and going like a bat out of hell. Pedestrians were scattered like bowling pins, until the car hit a tour bus.

An odd-looking man got out of the car with a gun raised. He was dressed in a weird T-shirt and dark purple scrubs. He looked around and ran into the hotel dining room where I was sitting. The staff disappeared into the kitchen. He went directly to me and put the gun barrel to my head.

"Get up, bitch." His voice was harsh, his words forced. I stood up slowly.

He pushed me out with the gun at the back of my head. We went to the kitchen where waiters, busboys, and the cook staff were huddled together.

"Where's the delivery door? Somebody open the goddamn delivery door, or I'll shoot . . . him." He pointed to a terrified cook who was still holding a spatula while a pan of something unrecognizable burned. A well-dressed man, probably a maître d' or host, silently walked back and opened a heavy door to an alleyway.

The gunman shoved the cook out of his way and pushed me in front of him. I stumbled and turned, gaining a step on him when he paused to see that no one followed us. He looked over to the street where he'd left the police car. Sirens seemed to be coming from all directions. He reached to grab me when I took hold of his head and kicked him in the crotch.

As he bent almost in half, he tried to bring his gun hand up to shoot. I smashed his head against the door we had just exited. I took off, heading to the street. He raised his head for a second and started firing. I was hit. I dropped to my knees and fell forward. Two more people in the crowd screamed and fell too.

The asshole with the gun ran the other way, holding on to the side of the building. As rescuers came to help me and the two other victims, the shooter had enough time to vanish behind the hotel.

CHAPTER
SIXTY-ONE

Carolyn Atkinson

Henry swore the trip to the hotel took an eternity. I tried to call Marian to let her know about the traffic tie-up but there wasn't any answer. Using the GPS in the car, we found another route. Henry was finally able to park, and we went directly to the dining room.

It was closed to guests. There were police everywhere. I retreated to the desk to find out what happened, including that a guest was kidnapped by the shooter and shot in the alley alongside the hotel after she kicked him in the balls. The clerk had no idea who the victim was. I knew instinctively it was Marian.

I ran back to the dining room and started to yell at Henry.

"It was Marian. He shot Marian. It was him." I was sobbing, distraught. Henry tried to help me and got the attention of a cop. A uniformed officer finally came over to see what this new problem was all about. Henry began to explain, but I took over.

"The woman who was shot, the guest. She was waiting for us. She's our cousin. Is she alright? Was she taken to Harborview?" I was frantic by now, but I had gotten the cop's attention.

He called over a plain clothes officer who shoved us out into the lobby. The first cop went to get me some water. We heard the story again. By now the police knew it was Marian. She was alive and was taken to Harborview, apparently cursing all the way. Henry hadn't been able to talk until then.

"Damn right. That's Marian," he said. He smiled and almost laughed. We had to drop John Long's name once or twice before we were given the OK to go.

I called Shelley on the way to the hospital.

CHAPTER
SIXTY-TWO

SHELLEY GARÇON

S am was a good driver. He was also very fast. We got to the hospital within minutes of my cousins. Marian was coming out of surgery. She was going to the recovery room first and then to a private room. Henry had called Rachal Groes to meet us. She was stunned at the news but joined us right away.

We were standing near the recovery room doors, now named the PACU—the Post Anesthesia Care Unit, a change no one in the hospital acknowledged making. Marian's description of the shooter to the cops made Rachal sit down. Purple scrubs, Omega watch, tassels on his shoes. She explained how she knew it was Nolan Herbert, and we all sat down.

"The son-of-a-bitch is out there. What are those cops doing?" I felt like I would explode.

Even Henry didn't protest. He knew how the force was spread thin with the officer shooting at the market, the abduction and shooting at the hotel, and the manhunt for Herbert. That meant nothing to me right now.

Carolyn and Rachal waited for the surgeon to come out, while Sam, Henry, and I went to Sam's car. We transferred the box I had taken from Marvin Winters' apartment to

Henry's rental car. Sam said he would go over to the ICU to see if he could see Rob Emanuel.

The ladies were talking to an exhausted surgeon when Henry and I returned. Rachal introduced us to the same physician who had worked on Rob.

"Yeah, and I asked her if she had any more friends I'm going to meet this way. Listen, Mr. Garçon, your wife is fine. The bullet entered the back of her right leg and continued on out. No major vessels were hit. Never hit the bone. Matter of fact, the bruise on her knee where she fell is the only bone injury. She's on antibiotics for the next day. She's already got bowel sounds, so she'll be able to eat when she's alert. I'll see you in the morning." He shook my hand and left.

I was relieved. Marian was the only person who could move me. I could be lethal, except around her. Carolyn offered to walk Rachal back to the ICU and let Sam get home.

Henry sat next to me. We didn't speak. Our relationship was peculiar, but strong. I nodded at him, and we sat and stared at the door to the PACU.

CHAPTER
SIXTY-THREE

RANDALL HUNTINGTON

I had a bodyguard when I was with the World Bank. I went all over the world to lecture or preside over meetings. I mingled with national leaders. I was used to being watched, but I couldn't tolerate being confined to my apartment.

My wife had died many years ago. Before then, I'd been comforted that whatever bullshit I had to deal with, she was there. Now I could only talk to a uniform policeman who was about the age of my grandchildren.

I was running GDT by phone. It was unsatisfactory to deal with customers, employees, vendors, suppliers, or staff in such an impersonal manner. After several days, Mr. Nice Guy disappeared. I've been told that I can be somewhat imperious. Just my nature, I guess, but I needed to get back to the office. I set up a meeting with the executive committee of the board of directors. I called Mort Jacoby and told him to be at the GDT office for the meeting. I instructed the patrolman to get him to my office on the appointed date. It was not a request.

When the cop protested that his job was to keep me safe in my apartment, I told him to tell his boss that we were going to the corporate office. The "Boss" could meet us there to discuss it. If he was late, he could wait until the meeting was finished.

Gail Jacoby was furious when she heard what I was doing. Her husband had been on the wagon for ten days, not nearly long enough. Mort, though, was enthusiastic about getting out of the house. His bodyguard had the same reaction as mine had had. He called the boss.

Long was furious. He was mad at me; he was angry that Herbert had vaporized. But he knew scum didn't simply disappear. It wasn't in Herbert's nature. Still, the longer it took to find him, the less likely it was that he'd be found. In the interim, I was closer, palpable, and infuriating. He didn't make my life any easier.

The box of papers and poison that Henry Atkinson had brought in suggested that Herbert had assumed a new name and was trying to get to Uruguay. The consulate was notified. There were ten passport offices in Seattle, and they had all been alerted. Every pilot from Air Germination had been questioned and their backgrounds checked. Several were checkered to say the least, and they were being followed up.

Henry Atkinson was driving Long crazy. How had he gotten that box? How did he know what he knew about this case? Did it have something to do with his "cousin"? Who were these people?

I knew Henry, had known him for years, ever since he and Carolyn had moved to Trumansburg, a little town on the outskirts of Ithaca. An odd duck, he was a patent attorney in New York City before he retired, ran off with Carolyn, and settled down. Maybe settled is the wrong word, as he traveled frequently and had a reputation, never verified, as an investigator who has killed people when necessary. He even had a Pancho or Watson to his Cisco or Sherlock, in the form of his cousin. Then he'll show up at a conservation meeting or write a story about a local baseball game.

Henry's an enigma. Herbert's a menace.

CHAPTER
SIXTY-FOUR

Marian Garçon

I was about to go back to the hospital for a post-op check.
Shelley hadn't left my side and was with me in the office
now. We had moved into the condo Henry had rented. All
of us were planning to leave when I was discharged from
my follow-up appointment.

After the shooting, when I wasn't at the hospital or
the doctor's office, I was bilingual. My dialect had become
pure sailor—uncouth, coarse, and colorful with just a trace
of a southern drawl.

"Has Herbert been seen at all since the shooting?" I
was getting dressed. It helped me regain some composure.
My husband didn't handle it well when I was upset.

"No. The cops are watching the house we saw at the
Agate Passage, the pied-à-terre downtown, and the effi-
ciency he was renting under an alias. No sightings at all.
Henry, Carolyn, and Sam are out there, but nothing so far."

"Shelley, I don't want to go until we know the fucker is
dead or put away," I said.

"I didn't think you'd be ready to leave yet. We're OK here.
Henry got Huntington to consider this place as part of his fee."

I looked around and shook my head. Henry had wasted
his time working on patents. I wondered if he could shake

Herbert out of wherever he was hiding. I knew he wasn't dead. He was a schmuck, solely concerned with himself. Assholes like that were much too fucked up to be dead for everyone else's benefit.

CHAPTER
SIXTY-FIVE

NOLAN HERBERT

I was sitting in a gin joint in Rainier Beach, leaning against the wall. One of the worst neighborhoods in Seattle, I was lucky to be alive. When I found my way there a couple of weeks before, I was still dressed in my tourist T-shirt and deep purple scrubs. I mugged a guy to steal his clothes, but I fucked up. I left him alive. Within minutes, I was the subject of retaliation. I was beaten to a pulp and left for dead by several associates of my "friend."

I survived, which surprised even me. From then on, my body odor kept anyone away who might have come near. I collected coins that I found on the floors of the bars that would admit me. I had managed to hold onto the Glock, which was my ticket out of there, if I'd had a place to go. Over the next six months, I lost enough weight that I had to cut extra holes in my belt.

I scrounged newspapers to get the crossword puzzle. It was the only thing that kept me sane. Some of the regulars there even left puzzles for me when they found them in the papers. Only if I left them alone, though.

I was doing a puzzle in the smoky blue light from a neon sign outside the window. It was from a flight magazine I found in the trash. There was also a profile of

Randall Huntington, the chairman of the board at GDT. When I saw this, I'll admit it, I went berserk. I began to scream. I stood up, knocking over the chair and table I was using. The barman started to walk over, a very large bat in his hand. I ran out into the street, waving the once-glossy publication in the air.

The *Puget Sound Business Journal* had an item that there might be a news conference at GDT and printed the details for the conference as they had them. Nothing had been heard from the company or its officials since the firing of the acting CEO, Nolan Herbert, on the grounds of insider trading.

There was to be a meeting of the executive committee. Although a news conference had not been announced, rumors suggested one might take place. Then the dailies picked up the story, which spread to the cable business news outlets. Randall Huntington didn't know it, nor had he planned for it, but he would be holding a press conference. I had some questions for him.

Revenge was Fifteen Down.

CHAPTER
SIXTY-SIX

HENRY ATKINSON

John Long was angry. He was still looking for Herbert. He had patrolmen assigned to all the principals at GDT. Despite the ambush of Rob Emanuel, these geniuses were going to have a news conference at their headquarters. Which meant he had to assign even more men to the presser.

Earl Sedlik was livid. He had been convinced that Herbert was a killer, and he assigned his best officer to the investigation. So far, a cop had been paralyzed, three civilians had been shot, and Herbert had disappeared. Now the rest of Herbert's targets, except for Rachal Groes, had decided to show up with targets on their backs.

I was intrigued. Carolyn and I had talked it out. If we played it right, along with Sam and Shelley, we could use this event to nail Herbert.

We were convinced that he was alive and nearby. He wasn't going to go to Uruguay without getting his nemeses. Neither the passport offices nor the consulate had had any contacts with someone meeting the description of Nolan Herbert or Marvin Winters.

As the activity before the GDT executive meeting increased, Long had no time or patience to meet with us. That wasn't a surprise. We wanted to go on record that we tried to get in touch. So, noted.

Carolyn had developed the best rapport with Rachal. So she was the one to call and ask if we could all get together and talk with Rob. I wanted all the insights he had. Rachal arranged lunch. At my request, we included her bodyguard.

Rob called Mort Jacoby beforehand. Jacoby was his partner after all, as well as the corporate attorney for GDT. Mort was ecstatic to get out of the house for the meeting. His next stop was to visit Rob and Rachal. He made sure to let it be known that he was on the wagon.

We discussed Herbert's known peccadilloes. Rob wanted to know if there was any way Herbert could sneak into the meeting. Mort was sure security would keep him out. When Rob relayed this to Shelley and me, we became certain that Herbert would be there.

Over lunch, I laid out my plans. Shelley and Marian, Carolyn, Sam, and I were going to GDT headquarters. We knew Mort and Randall. Both had to know we'd show up. Every employee was going to be scrutinized every day until the meeting and the subsequent media circus. Herbert was going to be there. I knew it. Would we be able to find him?

The baserunners were taking long leads. The pitcher took a last look at them and finished his delivery, a fast ball measured at 103 mph. The catcher had the ball for a millisecond before he threw to third. The runner was caught in a rundown. One out, a man on second, and Casey is still at bat.

CHAPTER
SIXTY-SEVEN

NOLAN HERBERT

I was high. I was invincible. I saw a rummy leaning up against the wall of a saloon. I watched him until the sun was down. Then I pulled the old coot around the back and undressed him. My clothes were as foul as the ones he was wearing, but he couldn't smell that any longer. He never would. I switched clothes and found a ten-dollar bill pinned to my new pants.

There were half a dozen cars waiting at the light. I flashed the Glock at the first driver who would look at me. He scrambled out and fled. The motor was running. I got in and floored it. I was out of the neighborhood within minutes. I made my way to the Air Germination offices. There weren't any police. I jimmied the lock and found my way to the closet in the back. There were two cans of 1080 under my desk. These two were the only cans left. I didn't remember putting them there, but they were mine now.

I washed up in my old bathroom. The sky was beginning to lighten. I had to get out, but I needed to eat. I went to the diner across from the airport, one of my old hangouts.

"Anyone back there in the kitchen?" I called out. The lights were on, but no customers or staff were up front.

"Be right out. Take a seat at the counter." The cook was tying his apron on as he walked out. "How can I help you?"

"Don't recognize me, huh? I don't blame you. Need a shower and a shave. It's me, Nolan Herbert. How've you been?"

"Dr. Herbert? Holy shit, it is you. What the hell happened to you?"

"Well, I've been preoccupied. Got any eggs ready? Ham and eggs, toast and coffee?" I asked.

"Yeah, be out in a minute. But you gotta get out of here. The cops cruise by here, regular like." The counterman with the matzoh balls went back into the kitchen. He was out five minutes later.

"Thanks. Good as ever. You'll forget I was here, right?" I brought the food to a booth and wolfed it down, like it was my first meal in weeks. It was.

"Sure, sure, Dr. Herbert. No one will ever know." He was polishing the counter and arranging the pies. All the time he kept looking out the windows. Some traffic was starting on the airfield. I didn't see any police.

He came to my booth and refilled my coffee. He really seemed nervous. I saw him reach behind the counter, so I shot him. I finished breakfast and left.

I turned around and drove north toward the Agate Passage Bridge. There was a large casino on the other side. I hoped I might be able to get some clothes, a new car, and a shower there. There wasn't a cop around.

There was enough cash in the register at the diner that I could check into the Suquamish Clearwater Casino Resort and get a room with two double beds. I picked up some shirts and a pair of pants in the hotel shops. I also got a lot of stares and funny looks. I made sure they saw the cash I was carrying. Then I went back to my room, showered, trimmed my beard, and took a long nap.

I thought I looked rather presentable. After dinner, I even won a little in the casino. The world was getting brighter. I didn't check out in the morning, but after breakfast I was fortunate enough to find some keys on the seat of a lovely SUV.

I took a drive downtown to the building that housed GDT. I brought my clear glasses, slicked back my hair, and entered the building via the coffee shop. Same barista, but he didn't look up as I came in. I walked through most of the company floors except the C-Suite on nine. Didn't want to push my luck.

The drive back to the hotel was quite pleasant. I stopped at a department store to buy a sport coat and tie. I decided against a bolo tie. That might be too extravagant. I didn't want to bring any attention to myself. I left the car at the back of the store and took an Uber to the hotel.

Three days ago, I thought I was a dead man. Given a few good meals and some cash in my pocket, everything was becoming clear to me. The press conference would be memorable. That would also give me enough time to get away. Uruguay might be out of the picture, but Nolan Herbert always found a way.

CHAPTER
SIXTY-EIGHT

HENRY ATKINSON

Carolyn and I were the first ones to arrive at GDT headquarters. We started in the coffeeshop on the first floor and worked up to the ninth floor, the C-Suites. We made small talk along the way. When asked if we were media or undercover police, we agreed.

Shelley and Marian began on the ninth floor and worked down. Sam Watlamont worked through the mail room, cleaning services, property management, and courier services.

There were two more days before the meeting and the return of Huntington and Jacoby. Mort didn't even go back to his law firm. Gail later told me that this meeting took precedence. What had started as a desire to get out of legal confinement set up for his safety had become much more. It was an executive committee meeting, a gathering of the corporate leadership. It was a demonstration to the markets of the strength and stability of GDT. Mort and Huntington realized that the morale of the company needed a boost as well.

They didn't want to stress their security detail too much, but they were stressed indeed. Several of the cops knew me by now. I was a friend of John Long's and the guy writing a book about the Pilots. I didn't bother to correct them, especially when they let slip the pressure they felt from Sedlik, Abrams, and Long, which came in daily calls for updates on their VIPs. I guessed that the only guest not feeling anxiety was Nolan Herbert.

The employees of GDT were having a hard time getting any work done. There were strange people walking around, staring at them as if they wanted to commit to memory what everyone looked like. We did. Nobody could figure out if we were cops or media. We said yes to almost everything we were asked.

The day before the big bosses had their executive committee meeting, uniform police began to show up. Some of them were brass. There were rumors that Earl Sedlik, the US attorney, would be there.

One thing was for certain. John Long had been there, and he wasn't leaving. He slept in an empty office on the eighth floor. No one saw him eat. He was everywhere. The cops were always aware whether he was on the same floor they were on. The air was charged with the electricity of anticipation. When Long came through, acuity improved, and senses were sharpened. Deliverymen were stopped, frisked, and questioned. He came across me on the morning of the meeting.

"Atkinson. You know Herbert will be here, don't you? You've known he was still alive, right?"

"Morning, Detective. I figured he was still out there. Something new happen?" I asked.

"You know the diner across from the Bremerton Airport? Well, the guy who ran it was found shot to death behind the counter. Ballistics says it's the same gun that shot your cousin's wife and Rob Emanuel."

"That's why we're here. I'm guessing he'll make his way here today. He wants Huntington and Jacoby dead."

"I've known Jacoby most of my life. Smart as a whip and stubborn as a mule. As soon as he heard Huntington was pulling this meeting shit, I knew he'd be here," Long said.

"When does the meeting start?"

"At three. The press will be here for a Q and A right after."

"See you there, Detective," I said.

Just as I turned for the elevator, a chill went through me. I called Sam Watlamont.

"Sam, this meeting begins at three. Anyone providing coffee and Danish?"

"The company cafeteria usually sends that up. I'll check and call you back."

Shelley, Marian, and Carolyn were next on my call list. Sam called back. He'd found out that someone was catering the meeting. The cafeteria wasn't making anything.

We made a beeline for the meeting room on floor nine. I called Long, who began to organize the uniforms. We couldn't find anything about a catering service. None of the executive assistants knew anything about it. There were several execs already there. Huntington and Jacoby entered together. No one had seen Herbert.

At ten after three, a man in a restaurant uniform shirt came off the elevator and headed down to the crowd that had gathered. Abrams nodded. Several patrolmen surrounded the so-called restaurant worker and took him into custody. The tray of coffee and Danish were confiscated. The restaurant worker was shouting, "What did I do? I'm delivering coffee. You guys are nuts."

The police, the gathering members of the press, and the ninth-floor office staff were crowded around the arresting officers and the handcuffed delivery man. No one noticed when a well-dressed man with glasses and a neatly trimmed beard entered the meeting room.

No one except me. But I couldn't make myself heard over the yelling. I grabbed Shelley as I ran to the door of the meeting room. Usually, Marian was the only person who could grab Shelley, but he must have sensed the desperation about me.

The door slammed on my arm as I rushed in. There was a sound I could feel, an awful awareness of something breaking. I pushed against the door with my shoulder, joined by Shelley's foot. The door jerked open. I lunged in, unsteady, and fell across an empty chair. There was bedlam in the room. Nolan Herbert was waving his Glock between Randall and Mort.

Shelley saw me stumble into the chair. Then he ran straight into Herbert, the two of them crashing onto the conference table. A shot went off, and the august members of the GDT executive committee hit the floor. Shelley had rolled Herbert onto his back and was hitting him with an intensity that I had never seen. Police entered the room and were trying to pull Shelley off the cowering, bloody Herbert.

Shelley was driven. He was yelling that this man had shot his wife. He was going to kill him. I staggered to the door, opening it for Marian to rush in. She screamed that Shelley was her husband. The cops were startled just long enough for her to get between them and Shelley.

"I'm all right, honey. I'm OK. You can stop," Marian said.

He stopped beating Herbert and stood and took her hand. They saw that I had collapsed against the wall, my arm bent in an unnatural angle. Shelley came to stand with me, and Marian went to get Carolyn.

The last I saw of Herbert was an image of him cowering in a fetal position on the conference table, blood streaming down his face. Shelley told me that two cops pulled him off the table and made him stand, while a third cuffed him and read him his rights. He was kept standing until the EMTs could get him on a gurney for the ride to the hospital. Three officers accompanied him.

John Long was directing the uniforms to control the scene, but he paused long enough to see Herbert being taken away. The entire room went silent until the elevator doors closed on the gurney. Ambulances were waiting downstairs for Herbert and me. I heard that Earl Sedlik had called the press out of Long's way and was answering questions on the fly. Did it pretty well, too.

CHAPTER
SIXTY-NINE

ONLY THE GOOD ONES

G ail Jacoby was in her element. She was directing caterers, handling guests who were upset about the seating, and directing others to Mort to complain about parking. Everyone was enjoying themselves.

Two couples were of interest to her. Shelley Garçon, who hadn't smiled since she met him, appeared to be enjoying himself. He and his lovely wife, Marian, were ignoring the attention she always attracted. They were seated on the second row of the Groes side with Sam Watlamont and his bride, Angie. Gail smiled at the sight of the Native American attending a Jewish wedding in the backyard of a Catholic family's house.

She introduced the Rabbi to people as they walked across the room. The chuppah where the wedding was to take place met with the Rabbi's approval, even though it was the first one that Gail had ever built and supervised. The ushers were directing the laggards to their seats, some Groes laggards, some Emanuel laggards.

The piano music that had been filling the yard behind the Jacobys' home changed to organ music. The wedding aisle cleared, as if by magic. Attendants and ushers proceeded down to the chuppah. Rob's parents dropped him off, and the crowd turned to see Rachal walk down the aisle. She stopped at the second row on the bride's side, leaned over to Henry, and whispered, "Do all the games end like that one?"

"Only the good ones, Rachal. Only the good ones."

THE END

AUTHOR'S NOTE

The woeful Seattle Pilots did in fact exist in 1969, though mostly forgotten. And they really did play in Sicks' Stadium—an omen if ever there was one. They were moved to Milwaukee one week before the 1970 season was to start with a team of seamstresses sewing the new team name on the old Seattle uniforms as the players went to Milwaukee for the season opener.

The players were the usual for expansion teams, cast-offs, wannabes, and hangers-on. (I lived through that phase with the Houston Astros.) One of those was Jim Bouton, a former All-Star pitcher with the New York Yankees. He wrote *Ball Four* while with the Pilots and Astros that year. It is considered by many to be the best inside baseball book ever written and is the only sports-themed book to make the 1996 exhibition of *Books of the Century* compiled by the New York Public Library.

Moe Berg was a genius. He personified "Good field, no hit," yet he hung on in baseball for years. When he was with the Senators, he appeared three times on the radio show *Information Please,* cementing his reputation as a pure scholar, odd in a world where no one else in baseball went to college. He toured Japan with All-Star teams, though he was never selected for an All-Star game.

Otherwise, this story is the product of an active imagination, a good memory, and some time on my hands.

PUZZLE FOR NOLAN

ACROSS

1 Arcane
4 Evildoer
5 Police
9 Extinct, flightless bird
10 Prevarication
11 Premeditated
13 Hitman for the elite
14 Dugout canoe
15 Deceit
16 Legal firing squads
18 King David
19 ____ instrument
22 Strangle
24 Double-edged blade
25 Pocket pistol
26 Nicolas
27 Bite the dust
29 Amateur killer
30 Needs a hammer
31 Professional killer
32 Smith and ____

DOWN

2 Vikings ____, pirates plunder
3 Rifleman
5 ____ made men equal
6 Nefarious
7 Debauchery
8 Execute
9 Victim
12 ____, toil, sweat and tears
17 Herd of cows, ____ of crows
20 Have gun, will ____
21 Why do they call it game?
23 Michael Jackson
26 ____ case
27 Murder most foul
28 Gumshoe

ACKNOWLEDGMENTS

This was a hoot to write. Baseball and my buddies, the Atkinsons and the Garçons, Bellingham and beer, what's not to like? With four fingers flying over the keys—(okay, two fingers stumbling over the keys) I explored Seattle, a city I love.

Writing is a solitary task. I got myself a new setup. Just a laptop, a keyboard, and a new curved monitor screen. Really cool. There are charging cables and a dongle but they just made everything run correctly.

Anyway, I was able to finish this book in a high-tech style. All by myself. Except for the aid, assistance, and shoulders on which I ride every day.

Many thanks to John Long, MD and Earl Sedlik for allowing me to use their names. I've known them forever and using them in my book is an inadequate way to thank them for their friendship all this time.

A big thank you to Milli Brown whose vision created the publishing model that works for authors. Many thanks to Dorothea Halliday, Madelyn Schmidt, and Kelly Lydick, the editors at Brown Books. They administered the editorial scalpel with the skill of polished surgeons, leaving no scars, losing little blood, and no whips remained in the body. Sterling Zuelch then gave me a hit on the head, which I hope to remember for a long time.

In the room, at the back of my mind, is the watchful Julie MacKenzie. This story is the product of my imagination, but whatever shine or sheen it has is the result of Julie's advice. The illustrations were once again done by Sephra (my dog) in her inimitable way. Not the cover. No, that was done by Danny Whitworth, with a fine touch and exquisite skill.

As always, there is Loretta, who never knew when we ran away where the road would lead. Fifty-five years later and we're still looking for the fork in that road that we'll take for the rest of our lives.

ABOUT THE AUTHOR

Ken Toppell wanted to write when he went to the University of North Carolina, Chapel Hill. He was there during a tumultuous time, the start of the sit-in campaigns and the onset of the civil rights movement. He graduated with a degree in history and political science before he went on to Emory University School of Medicine in Atlanta, Georgia, and postgraduate training in Houston, Texas, and in the army.

Over the next forty-eight years, Ken did his writing on patient charts in medical wards and intensive care units. It was a time when organ transplants—which were rare and only performed by celebrity doctors—became techniques which are now part of surgical training. Passionate physicians implemented new forms of medical research and brought HIV/AIDS from an epidemic with a 100 percent mortality rate to an outpatient disease. There were new tools and new drugs reinforcing why medicine is called practice.

As the years passed by, Ken began to give lectures in American History, and he had some time to practice a new kind of writing. He now lives in Plano, Texas, where he reads, writes, and enjoys life with his wife of fifty-five years.